*being totally mean.
You've made me smile...
Once... maybe twice...
Well more then that, I'm
Glad your in my life.*
— *Gerald C*

Don't Blink

By
Gerald Crum

**PublishAmerica
Baltimore**

© 2010 by Gerald Crum
All rights reserved. No part of this book may be reproduced, stored in a retrieval system or transmitted in any form or by any means without the prior written permission of the publishers, except by a reviewer who may quote brief passages in a review to be printed in a newspaper, magazine or journal.

First printing

All characters in this book are fictitious, and any resemblance to real persons, living or dead, is coincidental.

PublishAmerica has allowed this work to remain exactly as the author intended, verbatim, without editorial input.

Hardcover 978-1-4489-3843-8
Softcover 978-1-4489-3842-1
PUBLISHED BY PUBLISHAMERICA, LLLP
www.publishamerica.com
Baltimore

Printed in the United States of America

"Don't Blink, you might miss something." A catch phrase I developed from my own call sign. "Blink." My name, I say this as a smile swells across my face and pleasure is a sprite above my thunderous cloud of excitement while in conjunction with hatred for them and their kind. I say them because I have not yet been able to pinpoint what they are, where they came from, or what they're doing here. All I know is that whatever I am looking at, these creatures, are evil. That is the simple pure truth of the matter.

I can see these evil monsters lurking behind what others refer to as normal human being, I specifically call them hosts or drones. Not all of these creatures display evil in the sense that most human beings know it, I can just see it inside. Need I call it an ability, no, nor is it even a gift. It is an illness, nothing more. I hunt these creatures, this evil. It is my eyes, has to be. Something in the membrane of my pupils must filter out the signal somehow that disguises these creatures from everyday pedestrians. They act like us, is it even that hard? How can one person tell if another person is human just by actions, we all are bizarre in our own way. Does that make us all less human?

I do this job of mine not for me, but for the human race. Is it so wrong to want human beings to exist? There will always be problems and killing, but not from this invasion of evil, infestation of monsters.

I am considered in this world to be a vigilante, a common criminal in their dying judicial system. Some might say a super hero, or a hero for short. I am neither of these things, there is nothing super about me. I am not a hero, all I know is how to pull the trigger.

Let me set the pace. The year is unnecessary, years make no difference, society doesn't evolve from years but from knowledge and deceit. So, let me continue; it was a year like every other year before its time in the world of man. The economy has boomed to the point of extreme surplus, money became tissue paper. The ass of the country needed wiping. No one trades money anymore or works for money, we have enough, its now a society of "what can you do for me". Law barked and nipped at the street's heels but still crime flourished like an airborne plague in the wind. Depression and self loathing became a necessity, drop a coin it will stay. Luck in this world is a whispered joke passed on like the once racist comments of the past. Sex could be found on billboards and in children's hands. Decency is an illusion brought on by the founders of the past, those absent minded individuals. The code of the street is nothing more than whom can be killed the easiest, is. Morals use to blossom but weeds devoured their food supply and everything the average person use to fight for including God is now a distant memory. Other than that everything is peachy. Music, movies, television, and business are still chugging along. Books, hmm, haven't even seen a book in years. The occasional elderly woman might be sitting down beside a restaurant thumbing through the pages of a once prolific novel, now its as rare as a gem but worthless all the same. We do have a leader, his name is not needed right now at this specific point, he's been the leader for twenty years. His body will change but his face, that stays the same.

My turn. I patrol the streets, I save lives by ending them. I own two types of weapons, short and long range. The short range weapon I own is a standard no recoil fifty caliber handheld with solid copper HEX bullet hollow point rounds, my long range weapon is the big brother to my pistol it is a fifty caliber BMG rifle with seven hundred and twenty grain FMJ-BT ball cartridge. That gives it twelve thousand five hundred foot pounds of energy. My babies. I could take down a plane with the big one, I call it Sty, and its younger sister is Amy.

The streets breathe with me as I patrol. There is a bond, a companionship I have created with the grime, an understanding between the both of us. But let me start, you know enough about me right now. I am on the street Rong Way Ave. Yes, I found it quite amusing too. The night has just settled in and begun to stain the world with a colorless mold. The smell of the night is moist and the cracked street glistened from the puddles of water and neon lights lining the structures residing on the Rong Way Ave. I carried Amy. I did not know whom was destined to meet her tonight, but I knew that blood will be spilt.

Here is how I live my days:

The moisture collected across the brim of the night's steaming breath. A parade of garbage splintered the street as a heavy pounding heart accompanied soft rhythmic clatter of feet. Blink, dressed as a homeless person. He wore a collaboration of dark heavy set clothing, a rain coat, a black wife beater, and two pairs of pants each a different brand of black jeans. He was camouflaged. This way his memory will be as quickly passed as a raindrop.

He walked down the center of the road while his probing eyes dashed from bum to bum playing a child's game with each passing figure. Gently following each beat of his heart his right index finger tapped Amy warming her up so she would be at peace and ready to spring into action at a moments notice. The red blinking traffic lights offered a haze of solitude but also added a deep reverberating hum. The hum chilled the air around it tickling the hairs of the soul drained beasts huddled alongside its base. They are cattle of human life, the manikins of unwanted lifestyles. The herd grazed along side a streetlight's mount to the concrete below. The herd's actions are perfectly synchronized with each other, one creeps their head to the right the rest follow in unison. The heads together jumbled up a misshapen clatter of snapping and popping echoing from their spinal chords. In one gulp of tingling cold struck air the herd exhaled a long dreary sigh of tire and loathing.

    Blink in his disguise approached the herd with a strenuous pace. He continued to keep Amy warm, his tapping now in unison with his feet. Blink's eyes rose with the sudden cease of his legs as he surveyed the herd one by one. Left to right the herd jetted out unorganized sounds of coughing, wheezing, and clearing of the throat. Blink closed his eyes in a process he called "deformation". His mind cleared itself as he gave in succumbing to any outside forces. His mind became a black hole, a lure for the prey of his.

    He felt the molecules of his cheek bones give a slight jitter up and down, while his skin across the upper rim of his nose leaked a cold morose liquid. The liquid sprouted out of each pore of his face as his disposition became weary and sluggish. His eyes opened as his face quaked, the skin wiping back and forth adjusting itself to its new master and commander.

    Blink took a step back as his face reimbursed itself in warmth and basked in the model of its known pleasant facial structure. Blink twitched his left cheek muscle giving a slight smile offering into the wind.

    He moistened his lips with his salivating tongue with one quick flick, "Don't blink," His eyes surveyed the herd in a hastened slide, "You might miss something." With the end of his statement all the heads in the herd cocked themselves towards Blink's position ahead. Their heads leaned out till their necks became fully extended so their jaws could open wide revealing the decaying ash like teeth inside. A slow dull reverberating moan erupted from the herd in unison, the moan started off low then grew into a boisterous ear piercing wail. The eyes on each of the bums within the herd blinked one at a time each turning completely white and glazed over. The necks strained turning a bright reddish color as veins bulged and tendons bombarded the breaking point of the flesh.

    Blink joined forces with Amy as he rose her into the air to confront the creature ahead of him, each bum in the herd held hands revealing to Blink that this was only one creature but in the form of many, but without a clear defining focal point, he must execute all bodies.

The sound of six consecutive cannon blasts broke the silence of the night, shattering the moans ripping into his eardrums. The herd was nothing more than scattered pieces of facial tissue and skeletal fragments across the flashing red dye staining the intersection. The dull hum passed through the scene with an emotionless zest. A sweet but bitter aroma crossed paths with Blink's nasal passages, he welcomed the smell of Evil's death. Pleasure pricked his heart during a single solitary beat and then was gone. Both of his cheek muscles pried a smile into his elastic mask of a face.

"You blinked."

True Nature.

My heart beat is a water infested rag draining at a rapid pace. This cavity in my chest bearing my heart condemns each fluctuation caused by my lungs, because of my condition. I have a damning condition I like to call "thorns" you see each time the sulfur comes along I develop this minor set back for about a minimum time frame of a week. The sulfur is exactly how I describe it, its a smell that is a curtain tied along with the wind. Sometimes it passes sometimes it chooses not to. The real purpose for this sulfur is unknown to me, but I do know the consequences of not heeding its vaporous warning. Thorns.

Truth, how can one decipher truth from fiction? Fiction in some cases can be as real or even more real than truth any day. Any moment a beautiful array of poetic images could frolic into a man or woman's mind and take what little hint of sanity they have left and lead the manifested insanity towards the cockpit for control. But it has always had control. It has bore down and feasted upon the world in a hunger of infestation, invasion, our deliverance has cometh. Of course the tragic fact is that this invasion is not a clever deception of my mind, it is a clear vivid truth.

I offer a clear passage inward for the musky air of the night. I have composed a silhouette of screams and pain and woven them into a chair I call the wall. The wall is a place I sit to rationalize the saturated nightly scene I dwell in. Through a hole in the wall leaks soft bellowing breathes of woe from prematurely destroyed artifacts. People now a days I refer to as artifacts, objects for me to collect. Rare items for my fancy. This wall was created by me but me being the mastermind behind it no, it was arranged by another man entirely. He is named the Stuttering Prophet. An amusing name at that but someone not worth chuckling about. He because of all his knowledge and dedication to the well being of our race is under constant surveillance and attack. I pity his life but admire his pride and endurance both physically and mentally. I do this all the while tickling Amy, showing the gentle tenderness side of a survivalist. I have tried many times to sew these voices inside this wall but every attempt has shown a failure. I know how it sounds, I sound like my head is twisted a notch into crazy town, but allow me to explain. The sulfur stained a piece of unwanted flesh across my upper right eyebrow. This looked as if some black and white science fiction movie bled its gray essence. That was the first sign of humanity, our flesh is vulnerable to their methods of disguise, so in natural retaliation I first used the wall to scratch the seven layers of skin away. Using these layers of flesh fabric I coated the wall with a certain turmoil that I now regret, but we bonded, friends. I of course used the leather toe padding across the front of my left boot and patched myself up. Needless to say my skin grew one third over the leather combining it with my flesh and accepting it completely. This must have opened up a slight gateway of cognitive listening that can only be heard directly in the nervous command center. My very brain.

    The dew clinging to the musk in the air has collected across the exterior of the surrounding landscape causing every puzzle piece to be glossy and illuminant. I've seen my reflection in every object present, because each object is woven into me and I into them. I am the unsettled rage of the streets walked on pavement. I am the porous flesh of the trees leaves cascading much needed life to the animals below and around. I am the moons never existing smile. I am a broken clock in trepid turmoil waiting for an abundantly troubled comrade. I am alone.

My right hand fluctuates in spasms as I prepare for the haunting. This is a daily activity for them, or one I call "My Nightmare" without being asleep I see him. I witness his dreadful appearance time and time again while I rest my self upon this wall. He is not a figment of my imagination but a living being sent to choke the sanity from my cheese graded psyche. Preparation is the only defense against such a being, such a torment. So thus I hum. I hum a tune inaudible for human ears, it is a tune sent only to God. This tune can banish demons and crumble castles with simple note but I refuse to allow anyone a safe listening presence to my performance. The audience would no longer survive. I don't wish that on any soul.

A low rumble tumbled across the blanket of darkness till reaching Blink's feet. "He comes." A warmth vacuuming chill drained Blink of his prepared status. Blink's body began to quake under the cold infecting his appendages. His eyes fluttered down and up as liquid manifestations of his emotions congregated on the brim of his lower eyelid. A slow growing moan wailed from the wind as it encircled Blink giving off a warning foreboding the approaching danger, but he held his ground pulsing his right hand in and out of a balled up fist. Blink's legs became numb and uncontrollable as a strained breathing clashed with his eardrums.

"Good evening Blink." Posing directly underneath a streetlight was a seven foot tall bear costume with black eyeless sockets and a gray snout, its plastic teeth yellow with grime and covered in a polish of coagulated blood. The rest of the polyester hair faded from gray to brown but also dyed in the same maroon coating as the teeth. "You're looking well." The bear waved enthusiastically at Blink as its head bobbed up and down giving the smile plastered on the masks face a dreary insane flavor. "Oh," The bear covered its plastic mouth with both hands and gave out a jolly chuckle, "I forgot you don't like to speak to me now do you." The bear's body hunched over a bit as its head moved closer, its voice turned into a growl. "You don't have to worry I always like speaking to you."

"Uh…" Blink began breathing very heavy trying to catch his breath. His chest started to hurt and cave inward.

"Aw loss of words. Yes, the loss is wanted. Just listen tonight Blink. Listen to the sounds in the air. Smell the gentle flavors of life's torment." The bear tilted his head straight to the night sky and embraced the darkness as he stepped out from under the streetlight and into the street. "Most of all I want you to watch. Watch what you can never do, unless you ask me Blink. Join me. Everyone else wishes to. Watch."

A group of children hurried out from behind a mask of darkness on the boarder of a nearby building. They screamed in happiness as they lined up ahead of the bear all standing in a smile and laughter. They poked and prodded one another eager to join the bear in the actions about to take place.

The bear leaned over talking directly to all the children. "Are we ready to go kill ourselves?" All the children replied in a uproar of laughter and happiness. "Okay, now lets keep it quiet because there's a man over there who doesn't want to join us. He's a no good fun hating human. But not you kids." The bear's arms widened as the children hurried around him and hugged him, him embracing all. its head turned towards Blink still stuck in the morbid smile. "I've got their lives in my arms Blink. And you can do nothing of it. Nothing. So now you watch, watch as I and them have pleasure in devouring their innocent little souls." The bear turned to the children and gazed down into the mass of innocence. "I'll give you tools to hurt yourselves… or each other. Just have fun with em." Suddenly out from the mass of children rose a bag held by two older boys, it was a blue duffle bag with blood stains and grass stains accenting its inward materials.

Placed now at the bear's feet the bag was unzipped and the devices revealed to the children. "Exhibit number one: A razor blade, most fun with this is chewing it and swallowing it. You'll be able to watch funny colors exit your mouth which you can smear on all your friends." He handed the razor blade off to a tiny little girl in the front of the congregation. "Now the second toy is a hypodermic needle. This toy is a bit complicated, you have to first stick it in your friend and pull the end here and you'll notice some red stuff flow into it. Well its like a water gun you can than squirt it around tagging all your friends. Ha. It is fun, I have a few of those for you children." He reached into the bag and tossed a handful of needles out into the crowd. Children leapt up grabbing on to their very own as they probed the objects readying to play with them on the bear's command. "And the next here is what we call a pickaxe, cause you get to pick your friends to hit. Don't worry it wont hurt them all it does is make this little rooster cock-a-doodle-doo. See it on the other side here. I'll hand these out to you boys and girls too."

Blink rested, tears spewing forth from his eye sockets as the pickaxes were distributed to the remaining children. Blink no longer pulsed his right hand but now clutched an invisible weapon that would be used to attack the bear. Blink tried to move his legs but nothing could be done, they were unresponsive. Blink did not pay any attention now to the bear and his fiasco in the street but tried desperately to move from his position and do some kind of action to cease the bear's manipulation on these children. Blink grabbed at his right leg pulling it from its drowsy slumber as a wave of tingling needles bounced around inside his muscles. He reached for his left leg now as his head quickly jetted up surveying the scene ahead. His legs crumbled beneath him as he witnessed the boys and girls going at it.

With the same smile the bear watched as a girl coughed up blood throwing it into a boys face as he drew blood from a friends chest whom has already had his head cracked open from an axe to the head. The children laughed as some cried from being stabbed in the chest with the needles, but soon put out of their misery as an axe accompanied them to death. Slowly they dwindled in numbers, all covered in blood not all their own. The last standing boy tried to regain his breath as he looked about in a smog of confusion as all his friends lay about sleeping in funny shades of red. The boy glanced down at his pickaxe.

"Tag you!" The bear yelled from the sidelines. The boy's eyes glided to the bear and a smile broke across his icy cheeks. With a swift thrust to his head the pavement became his resting ground. He did not die, he convulsed and bled as two adults watched him with no intention to help aid him in his pain. He coughed gagging on vomit as he lost all control of his body functions and soiled himself while his legs and arms shook in a failing nervous system frenzy. Two tears escaped the boy's tear ducts as his smile reverted to a frown of fear and sadness as he died.

The bear stepped back into the light and leaned against the streetlight in a playful manner. "That was fun. I'll make sure to keep the nightmares coming. You know, you should pick all this up before your retarded friend comes he might just think its spaghetti, with lots and lots of meatballs." The bear saw some blood streaming into his circle of light, so he reached down and scooped up the blood on his costumes paw. "I'll be here again to show you some more fun. You might just start to enjoy these visits. I know you want to kill me, but you choose not to. In reality I did nothing to you. You chose not to stop me because you enjoy this. Deep down you know you do. You enjoy to see different images of horror in front of your face. Don't fight it. Give in and join me. We could have loads of fun. Fun, is what its all about now isn't it." He wiped the blood on the snout of the mask. "That is the sad simple truth now isn't it Blink. The sad simple truth."

Warmth swelled inside of Blink as he regained mobility in his lower appendages. His eyes blinked lubricating his eyes as the bear had left the streetlight, but left his mess. Blink clenched his teeth together fighting back any emotions that wished to escape. He controlled his body. Blink stretched his legs forward and leaned his back to the wall. A low pitched gasp trickled out as he shut his eyes waiting for the Stuttering Prophet.

"I'll collect your sorrows later children. Just let me rest for right now."

Their bodies are a scab across the tar, peel it off and watch hell itself rise from the Earth. I pick at it sometimes, hoping I can just pull enough to let the fire cleanse this land. Well at least cleanse me from this world. By the morning all will be unnoticed and unseen, a mild tampered rash on societies skin. Normally people behave selfishly thinking "I'm going to do for mine.", if their referring to their very own family or life its still all the same; selfish. If a neighbor is murdered do people whom known them for many years try to retaliate and seek retribution for their acquaintance's demise, no, there is no blood connecting the two. Blood is the defining point of cause in this society: cause for murder, deceit, and harm. The over stated statement "Children are our future." is nothing more than a cauterized exhale. Children can be the future but only if they are not contaminated by the filth first, if infection bares infection than how can we live without it. Time is just a prolonged wilt of all nations and mental health, drying the very fabric that keeps us all in line, but now that frail fabric has frayed and is nothing more than a distant memory.

I blink.

Inside the darkness of my inner eyelid I see the echoes of the past pristine and uncorrupt. They wave to me. They welcome their son with arms open wide and wishful. "Wish with me young one, wish for the trouble to cease, and we may finally bath in peace." This statement I associate with my mother, whose face in my echoes always remains blank. And here at this moment of memorable bliss I can cry, but not tears. I cry the only way I know how, imagine. I imagine a family, a family I once knew, but at the same time never knew. A happy family full of smiles and quarrels alike but separating the two and combining them all the same was love. This was my wishful thinking, my wish. I wish this was true, this could be the reality and my other life a false getaway for adventure. This wish died, buried away until the next blink.

Eyes open.

"Are you okay?" A timid feeble voice scrambled from ahead of Blink.

"No," Blink raised his eyes to a woman hunched over a shopping cart as she hid beneath a large raincoat that covered her entire body. The only visible extremity was her right hand which was pointed in Blink's direction.

"Oh, then maybe you should get to some place to … rest. Get out of this… cold. It could kill a man." Her fingers twitched as they still lingered in Blink's direction.

"I am fine, thank you for your concern." Blink noticed her index finger raise to the heavens as it quaked violently.

"Don't lie to me boy." She returned in a snappy feeble manner.

"I am waiting for someone old woman, please move on." Blink glared at her hand more intensely as he noticed burn marks across the back of her hand. They were days old, enflamed red and infected.

' He's not going to show." Blink glared at the woman as she spun her body around to face him dead on. Her coat covered her face as darkness became her identity.

"And why do you say this, old woman." Blink reached down beside him and touched an old looking duffle bag hidden behind numerous heavy duty trash bags full of random discarded items. He briefly tickled the duffle bags rough exterior.

"Because he's being held up," She coughed intensely knocking all her limbs into a quick convulsion. "The mart has him. Go, go find your… friend." She spun around in a ferocious zest as she held on to the cart and continued her slow pursuit down the street.

Blink's neck bowed over taking in the new information from the woman. His right hand extended towards the duffle bag once more reaching into its ripped open carcass. His heartbeat begun to escalate as his fingers brushed up against the handle of Sty. A slight sprite of havoc reeked from the first exposure of Sty to the outside world. All of Blink's muscles tensed up tightening, readying themselves for war. He breathed at a steady pace conditioning himself for an onslaught. His body must be prepared, so Blink continued to numb himself from any emotions his conscious might secrete.

With a momentous push from his lower extremities Blink proceeded to cross the street, the asphalt slowly exhaling destructive thoughts through Blink's soles. Without the slightest bit of warning a vehicle turned onto the street accidentally attacking Blink with its headlights. Blink stood erect pointing Sty towards the new object obstructing the surrounding world. In one erupt of thunder the front of the car imploded inward shattering the front headlights, the back of the vehicle blew out ripping the rear bumper into a metallic sparkling glitter. Pieces of engine followed the bullet out the rear of the four wheeled creature. The car slowed down just rolling towards Blink as his left leg raised up to the hood of the car to stop its venture forward.

There was a four inch hole running all the way through the center of the vehicle. Blink tapped his right index finger against the trigger of Sty,, while silhouettes of smoke trailed off the barrel. "Warmed up are we?" He smiled deviously wanting more.

A Stutter in Time.

"I have faith in misery." These words chuckle as they reverberate through out the vast cavern of my cerebellum. "I believe in misery because it believes in me." This statement I murmur bleeds unneeded enzymes into my body. Enzymes of hate, despair, and self loathing boil throughout my veins. The catalyst to all of these inner itches is the road I walk which constantly reads "wrong way." I wonder if this sign itself even really exists or if its just a mirage detailing the damned chosen path I continue to walk. God, he was real once. I remember his teachings. Most specifically I remember the topic or purity; sex, murder, all addictive by nature but merely a primal lust. He commanded us to rise above animalistic urges and shine out Godly morals and actions. I apologize but tonight I refuse to be human and choose the beast.

There is a tickle in my throat begging me not to go, I answer sternly with an apathetic cough of "No". My eyes stretch to the heavens while my head offers a just pleading nod, "its not much but its all I have to give." Proceeding down my eyes connect with the exterior of the Mart. A hiccup of surprise settles across the aura of the building. It is called the Mart because each human being drug through its doors turns into a walking pile of filth infected flesh, driven by an unseen force. Black and white vehicles litter the asphalt outside its walls as probing eyes jet out from each corner of the brick structure. Inside await numerous armored bots of "them", human stained but repetitive unmotivated monsters upholding their law. The hot breath of Sty's brings moisture to my knuckles. He hungers while I pet behind his brow. Tiny beetles of liquid scurry about the calices of my palm. The placid night continues all the way to the calm hinges of the doorway which will soon bleat out in pain.

Holding his head on a string dangling in the moon's florescent gaze Blink swayed inside the entry way of the building. To his left stood a woman like creature poised in an arch ready for confrontation in a verbal demeanor, not Sty's explosive screams. In a swift swoop to chest level Sty opened his mouth and laughed causing the bullet proof glass barrier in front of the woman disguised creature to implode inward through her skull. The cranium dispersed across the walls of the check in closet she had chose to guard. Before the first droplet of blood coated the manila colored tile of the closet's floor Blink had already removed both hinges to the steel reinforced blast door protecting the other so called human beings inside the main room of the Mart. With the fourth cannon blast from Sty's lungs the blast door erupted through the main office of the Mart.

The door collided with a desk currently harbored by a stressed disguised creatures attention. From the immediate introduction of the door to the false man's predicament the disguised split at the mid torso region and unwillingly clung to the door as it clapped against the burgundy carpet below. Along with the stinging echo of Sty's glee Blink entered the room with a stunning smile across his face. From Blink's left side came an attack. A desk chair was hurled at him. Without hesitation Sty's head turned to the chair's oncoming ferocious nature and disintegrated it with a pleasing whisper. The man whom threw the chair crouched quickly behind his desk in a skin melting surge of fear. Blink instilled a momentary chuckle as he destroyed the desk starting from the left to the right. The man survived the desk onslaught as he stumbled to a run from out behind the desk particles. He suddenly tripped across his coworker's severed corpse and fell. A toneless scream of failure blossomed from the fraying lungs which in one cough from Sty where now scattered through out the main office area. Blink gazed about and behind surveying the chaos searching for tools to proceed onward. He gleamed under contamination of his destructive crusade. Not more than a minute ticked by of preparation till he fired Sty into his arrangement of fire extinguishers at the holding room's entryway. The penetrating force of the bullet pierced both canisters all the way through both sides causing the gas inside to erupt tearing both canisters into a typhoon of shrapnel and force. The door to the abattoir of the Mart fragmented. Blink stood in a ready to reload stance. He only has ten rounds for Sty at a time, eight have already been fired.

Bordering the two worlds was an opaque fog of war eagerly anticipating Blink's immersion through the doorway. A small morose cough splintered out from an unseen object as steam frolicked away from the cove of darkness. In a slow playful manner the brim of a dolls head immerged from the nothing blanket. The doll's head swiveled as if swimming in the blackened water. Teetering in its playful glee it suddenly waddled out into full view. It was a two foot doll without clothing standing fully erect staring up at Blink. Noticeably behind the doll was a mechanical device extruding the doll's back and bridging the entry way. The eyes of the doll circled the interior of its sockets and fixated them on Sty. Jetting up the doll's arms became outstretched towards Sty but still far enough away for Blink to remain in his sweat induced calm.

"Welcome! Hehe, you don't like much people do you? Hm, I think you should come inside and play with the others. It is a hoot. We have all kinds of toys in here. Big ones," A whiny kids voice exited as the doll's arms widened to sprinkle a sense of innocence across its request. "Small ones, babbling ones, and some that like playing with sharp objects, some like hurting each other though, but its still fun just stay away from them. Huh?"

"Don't blink. You just might miss something." Blink digressed from the conversation whispering off into the darkened phlegm stretched across the entryway.

The eyes of the doll's made a complete revolution around its sockets as the eyelids shuttered up and down. "You don't speak to us that way…"

Sty laughed as the doll's head became dilapidated and sprinkled into the darkness in which it was forged. The doll's body quaked mechanically confused as it sprinkled its sparking blood across Blink's plain.

"Ha, you shouldn't have done that. Hehe, you'll be sorry. Hehe, oh so sorry." The whiny voice blossomed once again from behind the curtain of darkness. In a sudden snap the doll sucked right up through the abyss.

Suddenly the black flashed to red as the image of a man leaning to his left holding two mechanical devices wired directly to two four foot puppets whom were currently devouring a young man's chest cavity. One of the puppets had a massive mouth that when opened would fold the head back completely, its eyes were narrowed to an angered glare, also attached to it was a knot of curly hair flowing down the entire back of the yellow puppet. The other puppet was a girl with a shocked face of pain and its gray fluffy exterior was scratched away so some of the mechanical interior could be visible. The man leaning over holding the two mechanical devices attached to the puppets had himself a surgical mask on and a pair of scrubs which were drenched in old coagulated blood and particles of flesh. The man peeled his red glistening eyes away from his puppets and up towards Blink.

The woman puppet cocked her head to the right and gleefully screeched out. "Why hello there," Her hands clapped together in a muffled cushioned pound. "Do you wish to play as well?"

The woman puppet reached her left hand over catching the attention of the male puppet whom was jokingly trying to tear flesh off the corps with its none existent teeth. The male puppet gazed upward pretending to be out of breath as he too offered a hearty gesture of welcome. "Hi, hmmm."

Blink felt a twitch of warmth peel into cold under his right index finger as it pressed against Sty's cheek. His heartbeat crept upward into an advance pace, sweat accompanied hand in hand.

The woman puppet opened her hands wide as her mouth popped up and down bouncing to the words spoken in an ear piercing screech, "You stand there waiting, for what traveler? You murdered half a station of individuals. Do you feel better about yourself? How come we cant have our fun? You must come in and interrupt, why?... Why don't you speak? Do we ... frighten you?" Her mouth flickered in a snarling fashion.

"Yes, we frighten. Hmm." The male puppet hissed a quick comment from the left, "Don't bother us and we might not attempt to your ... hmm... you... ooooo. Or, else we talk about playing a game. A FUN GAME! Hmm? You decide. Choose, leave or play." Anger stricken jargon drizzled from the puppet's eyes.

Blink gazed through a bead of sweat clinging onto his eyebrow. The image of the puppets became distorted as the magnification through the salted liquid weakened and freefell to another world. "How about the third option. Lets see what this last round can do."

"Hmm, I like the way you think." Blurted out the male puppet.

The entire time the conversation continued the doll Blink had executed headless but cunning crawled now behind Blink until right directly under the trigger of Sty's. As soon as Blink spoke the doll reached upward drawing its tiny palm around the trigger. A deafening fear rang out into Blink's eardrum as Sty coughed up its last round.

Blink's head spun around towards the doll which was now standing knee high beside his right hand. He used Sty's shoulder to instantly abate the doll's miniature body.

Suddenly the light abdicated its thrown to the belligerent dark. Laughter twisted around Blink's head creating a nodule of annoyance. The smell of polyester and foam pasteurized the looming zest of blood and decay. This new smell pressed any button of Blink's it could, a child without self control.

"Giggle, giggle, ha ha, he, he, are these the sounds I should make? You step into my world and expect what? Me to lay over and die? I am the hierarchy here, you are nothing more than a lamb in a sea of sheep. Go back to sleep sheep. I'll be coming around your headboard soon enough." The light eroded the darkness away in one swift bombardment.

An abased gentle click peeked from the base of Sty, as a lone woman puppet stood ahead of Blink acting as if she were breathing heavy. No being was attached to her mechanical contraption it dangled to the floor dragging behind her to the rhythm of her breathing. Blink smiled as he turned his entire presence towards her.

"I reloaded."

The puppet's head imploded as her chemical bonding sparked into zealous fireworks for Blink. A scream blasted from behind him as the male puppet leapt onto Blink's shoulders. its hands fumbled around trying desperately to grab Blink's neck but Blink twisted his upper torso to the right and down throwing the hulk of metal and foam to the floor below. With the last sight of this being Sty's mouth open to a scream, the puppet patron ceased its movement. A high pitched wailing from wood scaled the floor behind Blink as a desk was speeding towards Blink's lower extremities. Behind the desk was an armless man using his swollen bloody knees to guide the desk along. Blink was impacted by the desk in his hip causing him to bow over in inflamed pyretic pain. The walls created a purl sound as the world seemed like water moving only in ripples. Everything within the room moved sliding in waves to the far left of the room. Alone in the center of the room was the armless creature laying flat on its stomach, its mouth jittered up and down aching. Blink raised his friend Sty to look at the armless monstrosity, but before Sty could dish out his judgment a metallic object pierced the back of the center piece. The man was now raised up stuck to the end of this metallic pole while a large dismantled looking hunk of flesh and steel held together in wires hoisted the man weapon to its shoulder. He was a skewer now for the mechanical beast. Blink immediately held Sty at the attacking poise while Sty screamed once showing his true power. The scream shocked the side of the spoiled mess causing wires and metallic objects to jet from it, but unaffected it charged. The creature rammed Blink sending him into the unforgiving air and colliding with the liquid wall. A chime of paste like water reverberated about the room while the mechanical puppet continued forward. After Blink's crash into the wall and kiss to the floor, he swung his feet around ahead of him also dragging Sty along with. Sty sheered off a heel of metal causing the creature to stumble forward and loose a bit of control. Blink swooped his body up as he connected Sty with the head area of the creature. Four flashes extracted themselves from Sty as glittering puppet pieces popped from the head area, mid torso, chest, and another from the center of the chest. This caused the entire monstrosity to fall apart loosing all its connective tissue. The man kabob was not finished though, he chomped down on Blink's heel grinding cartilage in its omnivorous teeth. Sty had an argument with the man, it was one sided.

Blink coughed in a strenuous coil of pain induced accruements. Fractured bones throughout his body poisoned the will to continue through the Mart. He tried to abnegate the warnings sent from his nervous system because the prophet is a necessity in Blink's world.

Breathing winces of pain shrouded the panels of darkness separating the meat locker from Blink's rightfully claimed room. Sprites of light bounced merrily from wall to wall as a hand extruded the darkness of the meat locker. The hand was coated in a grime and polished in sandpaper like calices. Attached to the hand came a being, the same man that worked the puppets, he guided a new figure steadily into the room. Out of hell's arms came the Stuttering Prophet.

The puppet master spoke in chords colliding constantly unable to find his tune, "I am not a fighter you see, I am a creator. My aberration from my fellow man should not be in account. If this is all you want, so be it, take it. You have no enemy here ahead of you. I am unbiased, unlike those creations of mine. They were under control by someone else. I just continued to keep them running… and happy. So don't blame a mere creator for what injuries you've sustained."

From his grasp the Stuttering Prophet marched forward unaware of his surrounding. Blink stepped forward and helped the prophet proceed out the building as Blink held Sty up towards the puppet master. Sty answered declaring his verdict as the lifeless corps of the puppet master flopped to the stained floor.

"You are safe my friend."

Three Goddesses of Vengeance.

    I support a constant anger on a needle point. Not long from now I feel as if I'll thread it into myself so that nothing but a meaningless emotion can take charge, finish my unmotivated pursuit. What could the murderous motives of one man do to a hostile take over of the entire human race? He, it, the man would bring death ... destruction, but not resolve. Could there ever be a resolve with violence or do I just add to the mixture, am I the problem? If I and the few others didn't resist and allowed the take over, would any be dead? Would anyone lay on top of the soil wishing to be six feet under and properly sent to grace land? Who will mourn my passing? Who would even care? There will be no proper funeral of BLINK, there will be no thought. To the world I don't exists, I don't exist. I've smeared the loathing zest on thick with actions of a morose nature. Sprinkles of salted beads congregate on my facial tissue. They cool me, comfort me.

    Right now, I comfort my friend. He tends to stare at me with elongated eyes keeping up his mentally challenged farce. His cheeks orbit beside his mouth as he prepares to speak to me, but nothing but dry cracking air escaped his lungs. This meant he was thirsty and needed some place to drink. He has water with him at all times, when he says he needs to drink it is obviously for a purpose, other than thirst. I make sure to take him to the nearest alleyway so he could be alone in with his thirst. I could hear him pouring liquid into his hands and then after his ordeal he hurried back flailing his arms eager to communicate. The liquid covered his mouth and dripped all down his shirt making a pattern, he must is communicating without words. He has drawn me a picture, they must be listening somewhere and he doesn't feel safe speaking to me. Across his shirt was a "V" of liquid, I could not be anymore confused until he started to pour some more watery substance in his hand and slosh it around playfully. I needed to go to a water source that started with a "V" or looked like a "V". I nodded also revealing I understood the message, Stuttering Prophet laughed slapping his hands to his knees in a fit of over acted glee. Then always to my dismay he tires out and falls asleep there in the alleyway, in the corner of the streets darkened eye.

Farewell my friend, till we meet again. That old phonograph plays the same sentence in my mind, over and over again. I bid farewell to this man too many times. Most of my existence is pasteurized in wanting, want for a friend, a companion. I began in this life alone, in this fashion I will end. Call me a sinner, call me a saint. Equally true the words stand on polar opposites alike my own self. I am nothing but a shared contradiction of polar emotional pelts coating my true self, warming it while contamination takes place. The right emotions take their collusion else where as they try to figure out the lustful ending of me. Hate continues to be a loner, the trematode feasting on my woes. I tremble with trepidation as I numb my senses.

Where is He? He's suppose to be here to give me cradle me and protect me from harm. My belief in Him and His majesty is decaying as I reek with the stench of coagulated blood and rotting skin cells. I was taught that He gives freewill and that is why we can choose to revolt against Him or be with Him, or even choose neither. I don't revolt against Him, I just wish He will give me some kind of seed to draw me nearer to … something, anything at all. I wont cry, cant. There are no more tears in these ducts, so I will submerge myself in a depression, the safest of options. I have seen the turmoil that the question of God puts people through. I don't fight it anymore, I just don't think about it, I try not to. its only when you see Hell do you believe in Heaven. I season my problems with slight blessings to offer tithes to Him, the nightmare hasn't come again tonight. The nightmare, it is not the easiest of topic to disclose. I don't know who he is or really why he does the things he does. I just know I hate him, if he is really a man. Oh, the throes of not knowing.

They spoke in riddles.
The three.
They tried to pull me down.
Tried to corrupt me.
Take what I am.
They succeeded.

They were three goddesses of vengeance; Tis the avenger of murder, Alec constant anger, and Meg the jealous. I found them on my venture to find the "V" body of water. How could my luck go so wrong? I've slipped into this mess with unready stance, equipment, and mindset. My venture to capture this mammon of mine lays in a field of cursed grasses and poisonous flowers which corrode all luck to the marrow.

I had been traveling in the cover of shadow alongside a condemned power plant adjacent the river, maybe the Stuttering Prophet needed me somewhere where the river branches. But without warning while turning a corner around the side of the graffiti infested structure I lost all mobility in my body and collapsed to the floor unconscious. The dark welcomed me.

I heard voices.

"So I brought you another one, this one was trespassing." The voice sounded weak minded and easily manipulated.

"Good, walk. Gates are present." A valiant commanding woman voice boomed from the left of Me.

"…pp…peel … his eyes open … make him see me!" Screamed a second woman voice full of malicious anger.

"No, why does he see you first. What is this? You're not going to be first it will be me." This next female voice sounded off in a pouting manner.

"Sss… Silence… you've been enough of a thorn. Sister, quiet!" The anger sprouted out of the second voice again.

"Hmm." The higher pitched pouting voice exhaled.

"Open dear traveler. Feed your soul some knowledge." The commanding voice spewed forth once again but now in a luring pleasant tone.

My eyes opened revealing three women, or that's what I think they were. I awoke in a shack, buzzing around near the rafters were three large florescent lights bleating a fierce high pitched hum. The hum proceeded to greet me while striking my nerves out of anger.

The middle one named Tis had no hair and one massive left eye while the other drifted orbiting around the socket. The left half of her face was smooth reconstructed skin that had become infected and swollen with puss underneath. She was chained naked to a wooden board with her hands out ahead of her laced to a sharpened railroad spike.

Alec, was on the right of Tis and she was covered in dried vomit. Her hair was white and thinning, her face caved in causing deep impressions in her cheeks and eye sockets. Her flesh drooped off the bottom mandible giving her a skeletal presence. She had on a collar which was chained to a metallic hook extruding the concrete floor. She sat on all fours doglike and unclothed.

The woman on the left of Tis was Meg, she hung nude by her skin from the ceiling. Her skin was stretched and pulled so it could keep her hovering in the air. Her hair was brunette while her face looked unaffected by the afflicting gravitational pull on the rest of her skin.

I polished my lips gingerly with my tongue as my saliva proceeded onward towards the bottom of my lower mandible. My heart bounced trying to push the body into cowering till a battle plan could be devised. My eyes rolled to each of their eyes, a bad habit of mine. I start to mumble inside my cranium egging them on to blink, just one time, do it.

"What is your name." Meg blurted out from the right of Blink, she twitched some as skin stretched to the border of the breaking point.

With a raspy reply Blink delivered a gaze into Meg's windowed gateway into her soul. "And how would this satisfy you?"

Alec's body twisted and froze militant in her intoxicating rage filled milieu. "…ah, do it, do it now. Why are we wasting so much time. Do it."

"Shh," With an angelic tone of vomited hiss Tis controlled the others. "Why will you not answer a simple request like that of disclosing your name? Is it because we should know it?"

I pondered with several clever retorts, juggling has never been a talent of mine. I blended all together intimately making sure nothing of importance was lost. "Normally it is the last thing anyone hears especially when I am pulled from a mission of mine from a friend of mine. I seek to end this war."

"Hmm, a brave one are you? I have a brave task for you. Yes, a very brave task. Do something nice for me and we will let you pass. My servant beside you, push him close to my spike. Let him bleed on my hands. Allow his blood to touch us all."

My blood hiccupped with an upset, I kill for the war, not innocent men and women. But unknowingly my right hand raised to the servants throat. I tried, using all my willpower, to break from this action my hand was compelled to perform. Here in my mind a war rages. Something is trying to take over. I see this Tis lady inside my head wired to the mobility motherboard. Where did she get in? I dismantled my thoughts so she would have a tough time reading them. But she continued to keep in control and push this innocence onto her spike, warmth ooze hugged my chest. I noticed the innocent eye of this being glaze into a metallic lime color. My hair follicles trembled in a beat like pattern to my heart. A boom quaked my body from my inner drum.

"Good, you are as acceptable as I believed. Hmm." Tis tilted her head as low as she could so her tongue could reach her forearm as she licked at it collecting each heat evaporating red bead.

"Why is it only for you! Pass some this way." Meg commanded taking control, while Alec giggled illuminating the room with a seed of uncomfortable sounds.

I witnessed Meg inside my thoughts her porous skin dragging along my mind's marble floor as she used her teeth to devour the pages of my memories, two and three at a time. My body started pacing itself as it crept closer to Meg, I noticed the cup of my hands cradling a pond of red. Meg's smile stretched far across her face making a "V" form as my hand's acted out of hypnotic commands and rubbed the red liquid across her face. She made sure to make me paint her entire facial tissue.

"You miss your family… you don't know whom they are anymore. You don't even know where you are," Tis' eyes rolled back into her head absorbing Blink's thoughts. "Hmm, you shiver at night, but not from the cold. From an unseen wanted love in which is never there. It can not be there. This friend of yours is the Stuttering Prophet. You don't question him and his words on the exterior but your inner demons say he's just mentally retarded, not putting on a false hood to shield himself. Who can be that good at acting? Who?"

I believed every word she said as I was spoon fed it in my minds eye. She held the gun to my head, she pressed all the button's activating emotions that have laid dormant for so long. I hid the deepest secrets away from her, keeping her chewing malicious mouth out of a box of papers she should not touch. It seems almost impossible to battle something within the walls of your own cranial cavity.

"When you're done with this one feed him to me. I don't want the blood, I'll take the body. I want his flesh. Make him more angry, do it. Make him writhe in hatred." Alec drooled a delight and blew it across the floor.

Acid drizzled from the skull and coated my headroom, I watched all my wants, worries, and goals dissolve. My mind was stuck in a daydream of celestial callings. I will die, not my body but my brain and soul. They are taking the identity away from me. Behind this normal exterior of a stern hardened face is the presence of a tear swarmed child begging for mercy. Screaming his last screams as all his possessions are stolen from his room, his life.

"I've got your whole world, in … my hands.… I've got your whole wide world … in my hands," Blissful Tis smiled shaping her mouth into a "V" as well. "Your mother and father use to sing that song to you when you were just a boy. Not in that exact form no, but I thought I'd share this tidbit of information with you as it leaves your world completely. Your past is now mine. I welcome it with forgiving arms. Don't worry your demise will follow soon after were finished dismantling your mind."

He's got the whole world, in his hands. He's got the whole wide world, in his hands. He, God. That is whom is referred to in the song. They haven't taken that knowledge from me just yet. It is almost clean, my identity almost entirely washed away in a vengeful tide. I see a "V" … a "V" liquid drips from Tis' mouth as well, across her chest. The prophet foretold of these three. He tried to prepare me. I must fight back, this is my mind, my body.

I drew a smile on my face while appearing ahead of Meg in a dreamscape milieu. Her teeth metallic and jittering as she ceases her mission to cross paths with the inner consciousness of I. Unknowingly to Meg her skin did no longer dance across the floor but had been looped to a ring behind her. Out from a page of my memories stepped a little boy who had a large extruding puncture wound in his forehead, he held a pickaxe in his right hand. His eyes bounced up to mine as he handed me the pick axe. Meg's face eroded to confusion as I showed her the proper way to dismember a memory.

On the exterior I noticed how close my body had come to Alec, almost in reach for her to rip my flesh to shreds and feast upon my entrails, but with the proper owner of the body now in control she will be able to do no such thing.

"I've got your whole world in my hands. I've got your whole wide world in my hands. I've got your whole world in my hands… I've got your whole wide world in my hands." I sung softly to alert the three of my domination. Inside my mind I uncovered the box hidden away from the three, Amy.

DON'T BLINK

A taste of mildew nipped at the air helping it breathe along side four other bodies. Silence cascaded in a whirlpool of intimate fear for each female party. Amy gulped in the fearing musk as she snuck out of my right hand pocket to say hello. I teetered my head from side to side basking in my cleansed mindset. My eyes shut absorbing what little pieces of the past I have left. I exhaled long and hard, "Don't blink."

There was no movement from any body. Each molded into a statue of faint understanding as it built itself with each syllable riding on each breath. "You might just miss something." I heard their woes exit in a lament of pure grief, my ecstasy. "Here you are. I remember you three. Yes, you are three that fight against them. You stand up so that the human race can continue. Your sign is the bloody "V" across your victims chest. It took until you drained all the excess junk from my mind to realize this. For your information my name is Blink. Something you will hear a lot of. In these days I have agreed to start the beginning of the end to Them. Now, you can decide to help me do so. Or I can show you Amy's favorite game. Some how she always wins."

Pathetic Fallacy.

    Blisters of annoyance and discomfort align the highway of my nerves. My soul offers grievances to those now deceased forgotten memories buried in an unmarked grave. Who were they? Who am I? Flames of failure cause my brain to swell with fierce acute anxiety and become intoxicated by the clinical depression powder that was mixed in the air long ago. They, the over pronounced pronoun harbors nothing but a clearly inviting blade to my throat. I've seen the silhouette of my death in the shadows of the dying children, and in the tears of the weeping adults. The citizens of this world curse me for I have sinned again, and again. I am the first to draw the accused card and take the blame for a free human's death, but I take the card with a saddening peace in my chest. I am bothered little by becoming the bad guy. I pray that I use to care, but I will never know. Three witches stole my past and I vow for my own accord that they will regret everything they've done to me; Them and the three goddesses of vengeance.
    I feel broken, unscrewed in a way. The mold of lonesome collects on my forehead reminding me I am and was alone. Have I ever had a family? I question the dew lining the outside of a withered shack. Inside the three goddesses of vengeance dwell. They have requested my presence outside for a moment while they hunger for what possible reason caused them to loose control, control of me. Am I smiling with

delight or smiling at all? No, I sigh knowing the three witches inside know where to find the central node. They, will know me by name. And that day will be the last for me. Pondering the freedom and the solitude that awaits me is nothing more than a blissful slap in the face. I try to push anything but war and chaos into my thoughts but there is nothing to grab hold to. It is all taken.

    The environment surrounding Blink awoke for the daybreak over dawn's chalazia. The sty prolonged the darkness for a mere moment longer till the golden rays enveloped it all. Birds awoke yawning with playful song as insects frolicked in search for nutrition. Life abandoned all fear and stumbled out of bed alive and full of excitement. The grass glowed with and inner pigment of lime green happiness, flowers prepared to stretch open and receive the lights ginger kisses. Blink admired the scene all the while hearing a slight murmur of music swaying behind the backdrop. The music was real to him and his needed break away from the darkness lingering in the bowels of his heart. His soul ached for this, he wanted it in consistency with his everyday waking. For these few seconds Blink felt happiness, he hoped this was the reason he wished to stop these creatures. Sadly he could not be sure.

    The warn shack door hissed open as a heavy stream of painful clamor exited the doorway. Blink's head sunk low with acceptance as he turned to leave his heaven and return to his hell. Stepping up to the entryway a toxin of bleach and coconut poisoned his nasal passages. His nerves screamed with messages to the brain, but Blink continued inward. Ahead of Blink were the three goddesses of Vengeance each still in the same pose he left them in.

    "Good morning." Blink passed them a greeting while the three continued to stay on their guard.

    Alec watched Blink's movements intensely making sure he didn't do anything rash, but what could she do to stop him. Tis gnawed through the air with her glare at Blink, as Meg chilled the world around her with her absolute hatred for his presence in their domicile. Alec's chest leapt in heavy bounds as she gulped in air and hurled it out. The vibrant noise from outside could not penetrate the acidic anger within the shack.

Tis started off while the other two sisters composed themselves. "You wish for us to tell you where you may be able to find the source of the Poneron."

I shut my eyes and absorb the request of mine once more making sure its what I want. "Yes." The three goddesses refer to "THEM" as Poneron, or in the Greek language "evil".

"Yes, I wish to know more." My echo probed the surrounding wood for splinters to hide under.

"Hmm, s...s...so you now choose to go alone into the lion's den. Fight for all of humanity you must? You know nothing of humanity. Why would you venture forth for a people that hate you, and don't care." Tis quaked as the aftershock rumbled down her skin causing her eyes to roll back into her cerebral cortex, searching her memory for information on the subject at hand.

I harmonized my tongue to hers offering a true understanding of her words. "I know what you mean. I know exactly what you speak of, but the one factor your forgetting. I am human. I can't tell for certain but I believe that all through out history there were individuals like me, an outcast, whom rises up from the rubble of his very own existence to reveal to this world that there is a reason to fight. We fight to continue this race, and continue the beauty we see everyday. I fight for the other outcasts, I fight for those who can not fight for themselves, and I will win."

Meg chuckled intensely vomiting saliva out ahead of her. "You, you are going to save us all from this tyrant? Don't make me laugh anymore its too much."

Tis stumbled back into consciousness after scanning her memory, "Alright, I have found you the rightful path. It is through the Dragon Arch and in the basement. There you will find your gateway into their domain so you can rid them from this dimension."

I surveyed the three goddesses of Vengeance one last time before I started on my way. Is a thank you in order? No, they stole enough from me.

DON'T BLINK

In the shadow of the shack's interior flashes of light revealed a chained up woman's cranium ripping free from its body, another danced the image of a woman's shadow tearing down from the ceiling and flashes proceeded afterward dismembering her entirely. The next was the shadow of a woman attached to a wooden plank, her chest erupted with a flash from Blink's right hand friend Amy. Blink walked out of the cabin calmly knowing his pain has been inflicted. Once Blink stepped out the entry way a soft whisper exited Tis' mouth as she smiled deviously.

-"Go to him, take the wrong path. Give my regards to ... the Butcher."

Hmm, the Dragon Arch is a night club in the heart of the city. While the city sleeps its heart sustains itself through the hypnotic rhythm of today's latest music trend. I have always known this place was a transmitter for the message to control society and any non drones, but a command center. This doesn't make sense but then again nothing makes complete sense anymore. I feel an itch of worry and dread, but this may be because I am heading to the command node for the entire invasion. I just cant help soaking my nerves in the foreboding smell of deception. This is the only lead I have, so thus I will take it. Was executing those three a good idea? My damaged fragile conscious asks blindly into my subconscious expecting an answer but all that is returned is an echo.

The street outside the club is barren, proceed with caution alerts are everywhere; yellow street lights and orange streetlamps stain the street with a gloom that frosted my own emotions with the same essence. A mix of electrical impulses and drums blasted from the building of interest. Vehicles were placed in parallel to the concrete sidewalks who watched me while I uncovered Sty. I made sure to bring the explosive rounds for Sty so that he wouldn't feel uneasy at all. its his favorite. Limbo cried a mist of confessions between I and the Dragon Arch.

-Don't enter. It is a trick. You will die.

I refused to follow any commands. I was here at the heart, or so I thought, wished. Sty vibrated from the music inside the structure. Sty warmed up with an inflamed hatred. His lusts are simple, death destruction, and mayhem.

The building was easily twenty stories tall or more and completely covered in glass. The supports were inside while the outside reflected the world right back into my face. The heavens have fallen for light fears this place, as much as I do. Darkness seems like an everlasting black hole absorbing the light entirely on this street corner right outside the Dragon Arch.

People are inside, some human, some not. There is no way to know for sure whose who. So I will choose not to end their lives. With so much muck I would not be able to pierce through their disguise and see whose actually underneath so I will just head downward into the caverns, the underbelly of the beast. I post three calming breaths into the night air as my feet clap against the pavement and my legs announce my progression towards the beast. Sty is resting on my shoulder saving his energy for later. His cool barrel is in total contradiction to the rest of his body, he is worried.

"I hear ya ol' buddy." My heart beat accelerates as my hand reaches the blacked out door, reflecting my reflection. I connect glances with my reflection, it pleads me not to enter. I refuse with a hearty swing of the door.

Inside everything changed.

People stood on a dance floor with their hands raised to the rafters as they all screamed with all their might, as if the floor was devouring them one inch at a time. The music was now just a voice in rapid succession, "Offer it, offer it, offer it, offer it, offer it, offer it." All wailed, "Yes." few chanted "No." Vivid dark green strobe lights punished the crowd as they began vomiting into their hands. Some ended up jabbing objects down their throats to commence the gag reflex so their innards could regurgitate their food back into their hands. Once they took hold of their stomach acid and half way processed food they hurled it upwards laughing and screaming with excitement. Music immediately kicked on as they all hopped becoming drenched with someone else's vomit. The mix of electrical impulses, static, and drums continued which shook Sty annoying him.

That was the main room, to the left of the entry hall was a stairway illuminated by a small red glazed light bulb. I noticed on the steps dried blood with maroon shoe prints inside. This was the way I wished to venture. I did not check for any kind of traps, I was prepared for their knowledge of my presence, this was the end of my road and theirs.

The first step down. Out suddenly from the ceiling came a body held up with fishing wire, it was covered in a petroleum based gel. It was a woman fully clothed with one good eye, it opened. The eye was completely bloodshot and the retina was glistening gray. Her mouth opened slightly as she spoke in whispers, "I did not like the mantle piece mom. Just don't have it there anymore. Please, don't… I don't like it here. Are you really going to make me come down these steps? Mom? Its dark. Its dark here now. So cold… I miss you, I miss anyone. Please let me leave." Her body sucked right back into the ceiling once more becoming absorbed by the stairway.

The second step down. Immediately following the next step down six mounted heads appeared on the walls, three on each side. Each head had their smiling lips torn off and turned around then sewn back on. Their eyes stared at me. "Welcome." Their eyes pierced into my flesh draining my body of pigment.

The third step down. Blood began seeping from the cracks in the third stair. Hot acidic musk steamed out soaking into my nasal passages punishing their presence. It was trying to make me flee but I did not. I closed my eyes and stepped down the rest of the steps in a quickened manner. I heard verbal shards of pain clapping firmly against my eardrums. Then everything went dead silent. I reached the bottom of the staircase.

A door of darkness stood in my way. A blank barren desolate blanket of colorless spears threatened me not to enter. It was a prism of unforgiving emptiness swarming the person's who've passed its border. I honed my senses, so I could pick up on any sudden attacks or threats beyond the realm of my eyesight.

Directly behind me unknowingly a skinless figure pushed me over the boundary and into the Butcher's lair. Here I welcomed the folly of my ways. I have placed my trust on a mantle of deceit and have fallen as cause of it. I waited for this, my day seemed far too perfect to be without a burden, my beast of mayhem. So here under the illusion of truth I meet, The Butcher.

Controlling the darkness held me prisoner. It is unshakable and needy absorbing your essence one pleasing breath at a time. But this did not last long, a sudden flash from the far wall announced the start of an old antique film projector. The slight vibrations in the wheel and jitters in the bearings of the aged machinery galloped around the room joyous and overbearing. The projector cast far to much light to make out the model and manufacturer of the equipment, but that was the least of my cares. In the projected image loomed a seven foot tall hunched over surgeon, or it was dressed the part. His apron was stained with the dried blood of past victims. He wore a surgical mask on as his upper eyelids were safety pinned to his forehead causing his skin to scrunch up at the brow.

"Good evening, shouts the inanimate object. Yes, I am talking to you... my next patient. I know you may think there is nothing wrong with you, but through my methods you will find out a lot more than you knew about yourself, entirely." The projected image swayed from corner to corner of the light prison, his hands rhythmically orchestrated his every word projected from his light manifested lungs. "Oh, don't worry my boy. Don't be shy! I will become your friend soon enough. Please step into my office."

Punishing the absence of color comes a dim blue glow from the far end of the hexagon shaped room. Now the room is visible, bodies of people bleeding profusely from obscure wounds crawl slowly and migratory across the floor without making a noise. A desk neatly organized with surgical equipment on top of it dominated the center of the room. Hanging low from the ceiling were numerous strands of meat hooks and chains connecting the two in harmony. An old phonograph record player started to spin on the wall closest to the Doctor, crying wailed from the phonograph. It started off slow and steady as it built up into an ambient swell of high pitched huffs and panting.

"I enjoy creating an ambiance of beautiful distress for my patients," the Doctor clapped his hands together sailing a popping clamor from the projector's speakers. "So you may call me Doctor while I'm on this old thing, but only in person can you refer to me as The Butcher. its a nickname I've grown to approve of. Do I like it, that's not a factor here, but I do allow it."

In peaceful bliss a blue tinted body handled a sabre saw lying upon its floor habitat. With a grin this body reassembled its face one by one grazing off the nose, ears, lower mandible, and eyebrows. In the blue haze the blood seeped purple, a dark black pleasant purple. Still the body crept on with life, but drawing pictures in its own life bearing syrup.

"They all try to do that to themselves. If its not hack it away, its grind or even sheer it away. I don't wish to murder. That's not my game too messy." The Doctor leaned towards the floor of his light induced world. "Can you smell me down here? I'm coming up. I'll make you love this room, I'll make you enjoy it."

The splintering sound of wood bending under immense footsteps chimed across the room over the woeful record. The room begun to ache while whining for its approaching master and commander. The bodies moping in the room shrieked out in numerous strained "No's". Fear melted off their bones and swept through their skin out into the air creating a dew of worry. The dew collected across my leathery cocoon. I can not run. My mission led me here, to face a creature that should hold an answer to … something. The worry silt of mine could not effect Sty, he continued to maintain his stern stale attitude. Almost ritualistically all the bodies scattered about the room rose up and stared directly at me. They knew what and whom was coming. The moment the far wall slid open with grinding metal and rust did not startle me at all. I was ready for The Butcher.

Prism of Malice.

    The Butcher, the only human being who can chop up his legs and still keep his feet. He was a portly man, almost pig like in nature and physical features. He wore brown maroon stained series 600 welding unigoggle with adjustable headgear. His nose, button like with flared ala and red inflamed pigment lining the dorsum. The philtrum stood out bleached of color and hue. He wore over his torso an apron of a curly cue floral pattern which use to be pink and green but now has the added yellow and brown stains of dried blood and plasma. He did not have five fingers on each hand but three massive thumbs and a grand fine tuned grin sprawled across his face.
    "If skill could be gained by watching, then every dog would become a butcher." The words exited smoldering from his acid coated tongue as he posed in the entryway. "Were you here to watch? Let me show you something."
    Overhead four 1000 watt lamps clicked on each creating 140,000 lumens, ideal for simulating the sun for plant life. The Butcher wrapped his disfigured palm around a cabinet handle tearing it open in a boast of strength. Inside the cabinet lay five unharmed adolescents. His callused palm reached in prying a woman from the hole and hoisting her up by her hair. Pain blossomed inside her body as natural

reflexes caused her arms to clench his hand and claw at it using her fingernails. Brittle the nails chipped away as she kicked at the musk of pain in dinted in the air. Without the slightest bit of hesitation The Butcher slammed the innocent woman down on an operating table and immediately using a dull blunt clever slit the medial epicondyle, located on the palm side of the forearm. This quick slit to both arms caused her wrist flexors to shut down and her hands to become decoration. He performed the same procedure for her legs striking the clever into the tendon right above the kneecap of each thigh separating the quadriceps from the rest of the lower leg.

"Now that you're here permanently I would like you to look at my new friend standing over there the entire time. Let him watch your pain as you experience it, but I warn you. If you scream I will only make it worse. So do not make a noise." The Butcher grinned gleaming his ecstasy across the room for all to absorb.

Blink could see into the woman's retina, her chord rang as he delved into her past. Through the connected visual gaze Blink probed around her thoughts. She peeled away hopes of escaping and summoned prayers to God. She spoke softly whispering her love to Him, and also cursing Blink's watchful gaze but that was before the pain drenched her. The pain embroiled her hatred towards the unknown watchman staring at her demise. He picnicked by her deathbed eager to cradle the last moments of her life in his starry eyes. A crunch beckoned a legion of pain to corrode her nerves. Her geyser stricken eyes still enveloped by Blink's stare, "I hope you loose everything you've ever loved, I hope you have to live with all that torment and anguish." Her mind cursed Blink in constant repetition. Three simultaneous pops created a stampede of color to spill from her cheeks as her eyes snarled with bloodshot wings. The tense nature of her mind let go, a solitude of peace and numb controlled her. "I'm going home. I'm going home." Her flushed cheeks stayed as her soul evaporated into the heavens.

Covered in the woman's extracted bodily fluids, The Butcher admired his work. He neglected to wipe the blood off his goggle and chapped lips. He puckered his lips to offer a gesture of love to his victim, he blew a kiss to her corps. "You were beautiful." Like an old muck infested wash rag The Butcher heaved her body off his table and begun to clean it of with his bare thumbs. His hands dug into a pile of feces and urine as he spread it across his thumbs and under his nails moving it about jokingly. "They don't offer anything after death besides shit. That's all they are in the end. Just a worthless pile of dung, the left overs of a selfish race."

Blink's eyes jittered back and forth swelling with hatred and wanting for lubricated moisture to rise from the ducts but his tears are all dried up. He felt his grip on Sty loosen a bit showing his weakness to his friend. The feeling of bees coating his face withered into his nervous system, his face begun to rearrange itself in a process called deformation. The honey of this process reeked as it dripped from his facial pores. Choking on this process each one of THEM have, he pinched off a sentence. "I am here to learn about the command node."

Blink's face spiraled back together and unharmed as The Butcher remained still and poised. A grueling inward intake of air surfed into The Butcher's lungs. "It takes a moment for me to breath, I do it rarely but my pleural cavity is quite condensed when I exhale. Could you please repeat what you've just said?"

Regaining his composure Blink spat energy into his right hand as he tapped on the cheek of Sty. Sty crept a smile as he welcomed the return of his colleague. "I have come to learn the where abouts of your command node."

"Ah hold on did you hear that?" The Butcher reached down spawning the image of the disemboweled woman once again. His ear crept close to the woman's once present mouth. "Yes, no what were you saying down there just a moment ago? Oh, ah yes, lets tell him this. No you just tell him." He held her out far beyond his reach. She was an already drained piñata, a dangling homage of aftermath to an undeserving soul. Her mouth drooped beyond her cheek's stretch capacity, she screamed at Blink with an inaudible fierce. The Butcher spoke for her jokingly mocking a female voice, "You do realize why you're here don't you? The Prophet sent you, didn't he. Sent you to the Goddesses of Vengeance then they directed you here. Does that not seem a bit odd that everyone you've met is trying to hurt you in someway? Why yes it does! You should go back and talk to your little friend The Stuttering Prophet now shouldn't you. But sadly you cant cause you haven't transformed into anything worth liking yet. So we have a bit more time together. YAY!"

The Butcher's liquid lips drooped up his cheek's peaks pouring a smile into the scenery. His enamel of his teeth were polka doted with black and yellow bodied decay. A severe mixture of disgust and harmonious hymns of poor hygiene paraded through the interior of the room.

Blink pet the chin of Sty keeping his calm and telling Sty to keep his anxiety at a minimum. "Lets talk this over. I've seen enough bloodshed lately. Yours would just add to the mixture but I'm going to offer another way out. Sound good?" Blink tilted his head to his right shoulder banishing any threatened misconceptions The Butcher might have had about Blink's attitude.

The Butcher gawked at Blink's cockiness and ego. Still cradled in his hand the woman was propped upward with her head chained to her neck cavity causing her to imitate a ball and chain. "You," He stumbled on his own words while being bombarded by obstacles counteracting his will to create words. "Ah!" His body reeked with a sinew of animosity and writhing repulsion. He in his stout nature waddled to the wall he entered through and slammed his fist of detestation on the metallic framework of the wall. He snorted with gusto as he exited the room leaving behind a dead woman and rocks from the inner cavities of his nostrils.

Light peeled from the room leaving nothing but the infected wound of darkness. The repulsing aroma of decaying entrails and blood squeaked by murmuring tiny little curses in the sanctuary of hidden comfort. The old film projector kicked on once again tapping and pulsating with the undulating image of The Doctor once again. Nothing has changed with his appearance as he resonated in the blinding beam of light.

"Ah, I like the way you do things my boy. Right now lets chat. Lets figure out what exactly we can do for one another. Eh!" The Doctor eyeballed Blink straight off as he stammered in his speech trying to control the hostility growing inside. "What is your name anyways?"

"Blink." Sty nudged the projector with Blink's permission.

The Doctor's hands spiraled out as if he could reach through the light out to Blink. "Don't do that. What the hell do you want?" The Doctor blinked violently towards Blink's position.

"I don't trust you doc," Blink placed his left index finger on the thirty five millimeter film, his finger blotched out the Doctor's image. Blink chuckled silently knowing he's becoming an irritation. "Why would you leave so quickly?"

"Maybe because it is I whom does not trust you." A snarl escaped the Doctor as his eyes darted to another wall entirely.

With gunslinger timing Sty imploded the wall completely sending shards of metal plating into The Butcher. The Butcher's leg's split in two causing him to fall onto his fat swollen hip. He laughed excited and stunned. He propped himself up in a kickstand type position as he also boar his eyes into Blink.

"Okay, I'm listening." The Doctor loped up an enormous grin.

Commanding and with the glistening shimmer of control in his eyes he pounced his words on the two, "Now the brains can meet the bronze. As you have both failed to realize my friend here has quite abit of power. Whatever sent me here must have sent me to die, but this outcome will not happen because I have come prepared. So Doc, whom do you know that you can get down here. To, lets just say meet in a casual acquaintance. Together you two we are going to kill a lot of people."

Malice Aforethought

1. I am the Lord your God, who brought you out of the land of Egypt, out of the house of bondage. You shall have no other gods before Me.

2. You shall not make for yourself a carved image, or any likeness of anything that is in heaven above, or that is in the earth beneath, or that is in the water under the earth; you shall not bow down to them nor serve them. For I, the Lord your God, am a jealous God, visiting the iniquity of the fathers on the children to the third and fourth generations of those who hate Me, but showing mercy to thousands, to those who love Me and keep My Commandments.

3. You shall not take the name of the Lord your God in vain, for the Lord will not hold him guiltless who takes His name in vain.

4. Remember the Sabbath day, to keep it holy. Six days you shall labor and do all your work, but the seventh day is the Sabbath of the Lord your God. In it you shall do no work: you, nor your son, nor your daughter, nor your male servant, nor your female servant, nor your cattle, nor your stranger who is within your gates. For in six days the Lord made the heavens and the earth, the sea, and all that is in them, and rested the seventh day. Therefore the Lord blessed the Sabbath day and hallowed it.

5.Honor your father and your mother, that your days may be long upon the land which the Lord your God is giving you.

6.You shall not murder.

Murder, in our judicial system is known as malice aforethought. I am sorry God for your commandments will end here at six today. I don't know if he meant to be as specific as those whom bleed red shall not be murdered, but even then I can not promise anything. The coating warn by these creatures tend to grow more elaborate with each day driven nail pierced into my skull. Is murdering many the answer? I ask this while I fold the hummed reverberations of God's commandments. Would I be able to fix death by causing more death. Yes, in all perverted honesty, maliciously killing off those whom oppose you has worked very well in the past. I can smile at the down fall of the Nazi empire, they were an infection that grew horribly contagious until everyone was burdened by their beliefs. This truth corresponds with my problem at hand. These things have contaminated the world, and I'm the only one whose fighting back, caring. I swarm the bodies of the dead with careless extracts of myself. My body numbs with each and every kill, "Bleed for me". I hear myself thinking such things while I witness the worst of human nature.

I want to stay away from becoming a monster, but I've already done so. I've transformed what I knew, whom I was and became this creature of the night stalking people that may or may not be one of THEM. I am overwhelmed with the decay of my psyche, as each monetary death nibbles and erodes my emotions down to bare a flavorless soul. Each death is supplied to and circulated in this devastated economy.

I remind myself that I am setting up a massive blood bath in the name of humanity but then the word of God rips in, "Whosoever hateth his brother is a murderer: and ye know that no murderer hath eternal life abiding in him. —1 John 3:15". Could these creatures be something foretold from the past?

-And I saw an angel come down from heaven, having the key of the bottomless pit and a great chain in his hand.—Did this happen already? Has the end begun and just left me and the others down here so we can rot with the demons of man's creation. Has God forsaken me? Am I to be forever a victim of my selfish lifestyle? I cant answer any of these questions. I can just continue. I will drain the hell from this world with two friends at my side, and their screams will echo justice, and condemn the wicked. I will show my malice aforethought. I pet Sty in a way to keep him alert but comforted.

"Blood will rain down my friend, rain down from the heavens."

Blink beat his melee of a mellow medley into the mind of the two separate conscious soul bearing being, "Who is first? Anyone really, just make sure its the most desirably dead. This is my gift to you." He collapsed his hand as he basked in the dim lit hue of the projector. Blink meditated there under the blanket of stern visual malcontent from his two captives.

An odor of sweat induced vinegar flooded the room with vigor, it first kept its amnesty until a shrill wheezing screeched from The Butcher's nostrils. He groped the grime of the floor with his thumbs as his pulsating arms continued to provide him security from uniting him with his victims fate, a date with the soul sucking bacteria swarmed ground. All the while he did not flinch one bit from his stamped smile which was cleverly directed only at Blink. Across the fringe of the room loomed The Doctor, he throbbed as if he had any life sustaining organs inside his beam induced form.

"I will not just divulge all my information directly, I will just notify you when the traveler is near." The dulcet words paved off The Doctor's words polished the room with a warmth of vile extract. The severing scream of the rusted hinges on a metallic cabinet burst into the room. The Doctor apologized with haste as if covering for something, "Sorry, I normally don't have guests around this long. Didn't know that would startle a man such as yourself." The Butcher had been moving without Blink's knowledge and he dug into a pudding of sponge like carcasses. Inside the cabinet lay numerous folded up human skin, they were all clean and kept well preserved.

The Butcher laid four human extracts across the floor as if making a welcome mat for anyone stopping by. Playfully he reached up inside his frayed thigh and wiggled his fingers about tickling the insides as they applauded his appearance with red lubricant. He scooped the blood from his thigh and sprinkled it over the skin's making sure to paint them with an even coating of brownish yellow to an acrylic red. The Butcher's blood compound dried differently then human beings, it became paint like, lathering and hardening without coagulation and decay. The blood was just for show, he felt no pain.

"Look at me Blink. Look at me." The Doctor paraded his words through the projectors raspy speakers as The Butcher waddled across the room with his skin moping the floor with his blood. Instantly the phonograph begun playing the wailing and screaming symphony, as the smell of sulfur filled the air from an unseen source. "I am not going to succumb to you that easily Blink."

All at once Blink felt needles sewing themselves through out his skin as the sulfur grinded his consciousness down hypnotically inducing him into a trance. In the center of his vision Blink noticed growing dark blotches devouring what images were inhabiting his pupils. His head rocked dreary and drained in calvary, filling up with liquid spores of weary contaminants. A rash enveloped his arm revealing the scene of a child frowning as he gazed up at his grandfather propped on a stake holding his own brain in his hands as it melts but he remains unaffected. He fumbled into this image as his body hugged the floor with loathsome hairs bleating in each direction trying to find an escape.

The Butcher was there to roll Blink towards the blankets of flesh. "Your traveler comes," Filling The Doctor's face was a smile, as it widened the light in the projector burned away setting fire to his appearance in one flash than he was gone into the endless dark.

Blink.

The world severed into two as Blink sank into his self-conscious. The presence of a young child lay weeping on the floor. He was sprawled out so he could take up as much of the nonexistent ground as possible. His tears collected and leapt off into the air soaring upward towards the heavens. They took flight making the dark glisten with diamonds a drift. The boy's mouth gaped open proceeding to call out to an unseen figure with the use of inaudible words. His head stretched from his neck squeezing it till his cranium blossomed with flower peddled flesh. A faint whisper tickled the timid tears, "I'll be on my way. I'll be on my way."

Blink.

"Blink, we know about your condition. The thorns. Yes, you have the mark. It is not present in a visual form. Well not to your eyesight that is. The collector comes to take you away. For you to become one of us Blink. Well one of us on the exterior, not interior. You will die. But your body will be put to good use." The Doctor paved his words out into the air as a haze of the ceiling wafting from side to side stained Blink's vision. "I'll take you some place nice for his coming."

I ache. Ache with anticipation and with a tranquil foreshadow of death soon to come. The thorns immobilized me for some time. How long I have no clue. Last thing I remember was being told that someone was coming for me as I lay, vision plastered to the ceiling. My body begged not me, I refused to beg for mobilization, I don't know if it was my strong ego, or if I just want to die. Dying wouldn't turn out to be such a hard act to follow, I've seen it performed many times. I cant tell myself that I've never held a gun to my throat and pulled the trigger but I can say that that would be the best way. If I were to shoot into the cranium there is a chance that the bullet, depending on how it escapes the chamber, will burrow just a few inches in or escape out the side causing; memory loss, blurred vision, loss of vision, or even acute anxiety.

Anywhere in the face a bullet will most likely just cause tremendous pain but no quick death. At least in the neck there is a chance of snapping the spinal chord so the nervous system shuts down and you will just feel the lack of breathing, while you choke to death. A clean death.

My eyes are refusing to open as my muscles abdicate any commands given to them. Do they know something I don't? My mind paints a gray color across my face muscle tissue, the color gray stands for sorrow, security. I understand my body's explanation for hierarchy but I've taken them this far the least they could do is let me see the problem at hand.

"Shake me, Shake me, God is gonna wake me, Shake me, Shake me, Refuse to let Him bake me, Shake me, Shake me, tonight we die. Tonight we die."

A string of song floats into my ears from a child's vocal chords. It was toneless and dull. The words felt as if her voice was a bitter flaccid soul withering into a smaller less distinguishable version of the former image. My eyelids still rebel causing a mutiny, my body sides against my commands.

"We wait on hands, and flesh sewn dreams. We wait while you, fill the woes of our streams. We want you to see, our enjoyable demise. We want you to witness, our children, and all our other lies."

Two cold dry fingers pinched my lids and cracked them as red filtered through the eye lashes. My muscles quaked under new management from an unseen force. My brows became an amebas as they constantly continued changing no shape ever took form. No fear, no worry, no anger, nothing.

The site I currently dwelled reflected that of a playground. To my right there stood a slide, but not metallic in any way. It was made entirely of fingers, severed and sewn. Below it the outline of a hopscotch painted with a yellowish brown mucus, each square containing footprints of coagulated blood. Directly opposite of the two toys to my left there was a jungle gym. The gym was made entirely of hair, woven black hair. Beside the jungle gym hunched over in a semicircle were children. Their mouths were open as they gnawed at their fingers tearing the flesh and muscle off the tips and leaving a hole, no blood exited their self inflicted wounds.

A little girl snapped her head back and forth cracking every vertebrae in her spinal chord, as she connected eyes with me. Her face blushed with excitement as her body remained in a gray scale of darkening colors. "All done." She held her hand out completely revealing each of her finger's tips which had the finger prints gnawed completely out and the only thing left was a fingernail and a skin outline.

All the children wore old fifties attire. Their hair also combed in the sitcom fifties style as well, but a boy stood out as his hair was combed in a greaser fashion. The children were all drained of color and intensely finishing their chewing homework.

After the little girl the greaser finished his work proudly wobbling his palms for all the other pose of children to see. A few other children ceased their chewing to marvel in amazement at the boy's accomplishment. The girl crouched next to the greaser raised her only devoured finger and positioned it towards the little boy's face. The greaser puckered up his death entranced lips and blew sporadic gusts of musk into her hollowed out tip, she giggled with utter delight.

Even if the children haven't finished their work the greaser erected himself in the middle of the semicircle and without any noises or words he nodded towards the jungle gym of hair. Four of the children plopped their little butts of ecstasy into a liquid of pure rampage as they coughed in laughter all the way to the jungle gym's base. Each child touched the hair and immediately the brunette wads intertwined with the children's hollowed finger tips. One child convulsed as he became feverishly ill, he sprouted into a sweat fountain as his body broke into pieces and became putty in the hair's control. The boys body molded itself into the base of a seesaw. The other children accompanied this boy as the same incident repeated itself. A full child built seesaw convened beside the jungle gym.

The greaser giggled with enthusiastic delight as he watched the other children get their bodies serrated and poised into a swing set, their small intestines serving as the chains connecting the hipbone seats. Blood did not exit the children at all.

The greaser pried his eyes from the new toys in this park and peeled the visual scab which was me laying on the gray stained gravel. Behind the greaser appeared a fourteen foot chain link fence and blackening clouds over head. Like any little child would seeing a stranger near him, he smiled and waved overjoyed. "Did you see how much fun they had?" His hands fluttered ahead of himself. "Oh, I'm sorry let me allow you to speak."

My body rotated to my side in an uncontrollable furry as I exhaled a gallon of blood onto the gray gravel. I coughed someone else's confusion as the blood soaked into the sponge like gravel. "Blood?" I choked out while spitting the last remains of red lavished lubricant.

"Jee, didn't you wonder why none of my classmates bled? I used it to keep you in bondage." The greaser chuckled as he offered a smile of sarcasm and pleased fortitude. "These ankle-bitters went ape as I showed the cubes my jets, so they wouldn't be so ... square. Hmm so oddball you have received the royal shaft now have you, my grody man? I see your abit on the stick right now so here let me get you in orbit, your in my pad. I'm a bit subterranean so don't rip on the threads. My names Cold. Now to you. You look like a wet rag. Why would my radioactive friend Butch be tight with you? Or are you two abit frosted with each other? Now you know I get pretty razzed when people anger my friends, get with it?"

My teeth were laced with the ruminants of the children's blood, "You can stop with the fifties slang. There's no one else here but me. Reveal yourself and stop hiding in this little kid's body. This is a pathetic meandering from someone who is obviously much more capable then meets the eye. So lets not talk about The Butcher, or Butch as you refer to it as, and lets really delve into the straight stern fact. I am here, your pad. Why? What do you plan for me?" Tremors ransack my hunched figure with forsaken promises as they try to prepare my flesh for the mortal decay of death.

The greaser blinked snarling through the colorless coating of his. "What are you writing a book? I sensed you were bad news when you got here. You wont fit into my playground." A seismic wave pummeled his little adolescent head as he lashed his tongue out flailing his scalp left and right fighting off an invisible foe. In a bipolar snap the greaser returned to his calm cool self. "You bug me. But let me tell you something big daddy. You and I we are nothing in this scene. You think you've done any good. You've just had a blast killing, that's all. Try to cast an eyeball over your life, what do you see? You've cranked up the city but you've gut the gas on any good you've done. That messed up prophet must have sent you out? This isn't the made in the shade adventure you hoped it to be, is it? You should learn to pile up some Z's before you come pounding on the big dog's door."

Tendrils of laughter sprout from Blink as he takes his left thumb to his fangs. Chomping into the seven layers of flesh his right canine pierced the bone accompanying the marrow inside. Blood cascaded down his stretched cheek cells as it offered its soul to the gravel below. The deception of enjoyment reverberated from Blink's face as he tore into his thumb's heart.

"No! Stop it! I don't want you apart of my family. You've been clutched! Stop it!" The greaser flaunted his fingers ahead of him revealing his hollow fingertips, as they proceeded to holster Blink's rampage on his thumb. The greaser wrapped his palms around Blink's left wrist and rocketed the thumb out from Blink's bite radius.

A hazed smile infected Blink's cheeks as he caught the greaser in a choke hold with his right hand and squeezed its trachea till no particle of air could pass. Blink raised from the gravel of the playground's floor still grasping the child's throat with all his might. The greaser's hands pounded rhythmically on Blink's forearm as it desperately tried to escape. "Let me tell you a story of a young boy who didn't tell a stranger what he wanted to know. Blink twice for me if you don't want to hear this story and I can trust you, and let you down." The greaser blinked rapidly pleading to be let down. Blink let the boy go as tremendous vacuums of air spiraled into the boy's lungs. "So I know your names not Cold. What is it?"

The adolescent coughed spilling liquid emotion from his tear ducts. "its Theodore." He gulped down saliva in the form of lubricating salvation. His face winced with every retraction of his windpipe.

Blink's right palm comforted Theodore's scalp as he apologized through touch. "Are you human?"

Theodore pulled back to save his gelled hair from being ruined, "That's a stupid question to ask, Einstein."

Blink compiled a nice hearty air intake for his lungs, "So how much do you know?" Blink gazed down at the tiny figure of Theodore's.

Theodore glared upward upset and uneasy, "Everything, just about everything, and everyone."

Blink smiled wide suffocating the surroundings making it void of all woe, "Good, now lets make you more travel friendly."

Theodore tried to fight Blink's hands off his head but it was no use, Blink held tight and with a few clockwise twists he disconnected Theodore's head from his body. Theodore screamed into the abyss of the playground's emotionless hue. A bloodless body lay sprawled out on the playground's gravel as Theodore's head was hoisted directly ahead of Blink's face.

Theodore frowned in a meaningless pounce of anger, "You are an asshole! Your really gone man! Really, really gone!"

Blink's face gleamed in a serious coating, "Where are my guns?"

Theodore pranced his eyes about his sockets in momentary bliss, "Still Butch, or the butcher has them. And if I don't tell them I've killed you in about half an hour, your time. Then, they will send the reinforcements. You really don't want…"

Blink pressed his left hand over Theodore's mouth with great force, "Don't worry, were going to get my guns." He uncovered Theodore's mouth as he paused in a swarm of silence. "We will start a war."

WAR.

My face melts with the sadness empowering my heart. Some how it continues its crippling compulsion to maintain my life's onward progression through a world banished into turmoil. The meaningless ash of my dreams, emotions, and thoughts flutter away into the wind. Faith of those few pieces returning are limited. I feel the pasteurizing glare of God's on my cheeks, but I feel condemned. My body pants with the blood of ache and tire. I reject any plea of recession or halt from my flesh.

"Boss! This is pretty far out man. Never thought I'd be betraying my own kind and carried around all in one day." Theodore jabbered on from beneath my armpit. I held his cranium with my right arm as I surveyed the land, his home.

"What is this place?" I generated curiosity as I watched translucent specters floating merrily from the cloud infested heaven's above. They drizzled down wafting around the playground in a snowflake fashion. When these specters reached the end of their travel a low pitched hiss would envelope the air momentarily but in a music tempo with the other specters performing the same routine.

'Well boss its where the souls come to weep, because of their passing." Theodore's head wiggled with frustration of being only a head.

I felt a tear creep to the side of my right eye socket. This was new for me, feeling anything. Hallelujah. I am a composed but broken Hallelujah. My body drips the hallelujah on to a world that burned it. I'm drained of all hallelujah, a shriveling leaf on a dying tree. There might be something else to me, why am I still alive? How do I continue on? I am a purpose, I am an understanding. I don't believe I understand what I am doing but I will follow it. That is my hallelujah.

"This is a highway of the damned?" The pressure of my eyelid squeezed the single drop of emotion out of my sight and into oblivion.

"Ah ha, you know some of your stuff. That's correct o boss. I live in the highway. Right under this playground here is a disposal unit that collects these souls and manufactures them into… I dunno, tea cups?" A spirit passed right in front of Theodore as he tried to stick his tongue out and touch it while it wept into the gravel. "You know you could just put me in the path of a few of these, it rocks your world being inside one as it drops."

"Quiet." I loosened some of Theodore's gelled hair and tied it together into a handle for carrying his eight pound cranium. "There, that's better."

"Why the heck did you do that?" With a quick lunge Theodore's chin collided with the slide of fingers and slid its way down to the gravel. He moaned a stench of filth injected hatred all the way down the slide. "You slime ball. What am I now your talking purse?"

"When I say shut up, you shut up. Think of that as a test for what can and will happen., a lot. And if you keep it up, it will just get better and better." A devious grin of mine gathered up all the bewildered gazes of Theodore's.

"You're a freaking mental case. You do know that right?" Theodore's lower mandible snapped back and forth as he spoke making his head appear to be jumping up and down.

"I've survived this long," I scooped up the jabbering remains of Theodore. "How do we get out of this place?"

Theodore's voice was muffled from the fabric of my clothing sinking into this left cheek's comfort. "You cant leave until the next morning, only when the sun reaches the mirror can we exit the playground."

A plight of annoyance interlaced itself with my eardrums, "What is this some kind of riddle. Just show me where the exit is."

"TO YOUR RIGHT, BOSS." His words itched into my nerves. A spore of sincere apologetic sincerity wiped my face clean as I cocked my head towards a six foot freestanding mirror.

The malevolent radiance from the cloud's luminescent glow outlined my image that presented itself ahead of me in the mirror. I wonder why the mirror chose to reveal such a burdened wretch of a soul, but not Theodore. My countenance beside the mirror's likeness of me seemed almost misshapen and ameba like. I feel placid, invisible and forged in an unstructured plasma. Here I see myself. I've reached the finish line, but haven't all at once.

The cool drips of sweat bead up across my face as a heavenly gold encompasses my face gently kissing each crying pore. The warmth of this sudden gold draws the anger from my cheeks and absorbs all negativity. I am at peace. Just as quick as it arrived the gold dropped and now my face cracked under the dry gray dislocated hell. The sadness and seclusion of my emotions continued once more galloping into a hopeless stricken folly.

"You experienced one. How did it feel? Yeah, they are pretty addictive, boss. Next time maybe you could share. They are always falling around here just maybe pass me around some, hell you can roll me if you would like." Theodore's eyes flicked in unison at me as I recovered from my spiral into another domain.

"I liked it." I frolicked in the burdening folly I was struck with. This persistent jabbering head plucked the correct chords with his tongue, I am wanting more. My face blisters red as I sail away with anger from my instant addiction. Do I romp in the sin of absorbing other people's souls or do I lather my mouth with red liquid from my lower lip and continue the bordering impossible campaign of mine? I don't know. My morality meter has all but dropped down to devils advocate but still I plead to push the heavenly aspect on to the rest of the world, even though I fail miserably. I cringe as I breathe because a soul drops now ahead of me from the gray scale sky. I clench. Goodbye, goodbye.

Theodore slid a snakelike smile across his face, "Okay boss, okay. Sit in front of this mirror. We will be back soon enough."

I cooperated with the head as I crossed my legs then closing my eyes sorrow suddenly peeled from my skin. The shavings of sorrow spiraled into words as I spoke. "Do you believe we can get through this? I don't get why you, your kind has to take over. There could have been peace."

Theodore pinched his cheek against my ribcage, "You don't get it. We have seen your kind. This is the best way for peace. Annihilation. That is peace. Your kind can not understand true peace, you can not even understand not to murder your own kind. What difference are we making in your little old lives? We are doing exactly what you were all doing, but we are doing it behind a mask. Smarter tactics."

I clamped my teeth around my own image as the mirror beamed the atrocity back into my face, "What gives your kind the right to say were lesser beings. Our differences don't out weigh our likeness."

Beatty little black pupils relayed their glare off the mirror and into my eyes from an object that in normal terms should be deceased. "Hardy har harr. You are tugging on the likeness card. We, as a civilization try not to unfold our plans to something far more inferior to us. You have no idea what we are capable of."

The image of mine screwed a morbid smile onto its face as it drooled the flesh away and now left was a grinning demon of wrath. "Eye for eye, tooth for tooth, hand for hand, foot for foot, burn for burn, wound for wound, stripe for stripe. Exodus."

"Huh?" The coils of Theodore's confusion snapped and struck him with dumbfounded awe.

I rose glaring deep into the barren cavity of my own image. "Today dear head you will see the extent of our inferior race. You may think it primitive but I assure you we are far more better at it then your kind. It is time for the war."

I hurled the head through a wallowing spirit descending into the damned core of the world. The head connected spitefully with the liquid glass of the mirror and splashed its remains across the gray pavement. Holstered ahead of me stood a doorway, handle and all. Theodore rang a thud from the wooden exterior and paraded across the floor until I scooped him up again. His face swelled with anger and trepidation.

I placed my hand upon the door and turned the knob of desolation. "Revelation 11:7

And when they have finished their testimony, the beast that rises from the bottomless pit will make war on them and conquer them and kill them. I am this beast."

I cant say that it didn't take long or even say that it was quick getting here, but I found my way out of this hole. Apparently Theodore lived in a basement underneath a grocery store that has long since been demolished. It took me crawling on my hands and knees to push up through the tight cavern leading down into Theodore's hovel, so venturing into the dilapidated store seemed logical enough to get cleaned up or to equip myself.

Convenient stores can be so convenient for any need. Happily I found they had a cologne department along with the glass bottles of energy drinks or coke products, I made myself three nice Molotov cocktails. I found a leather glove that covered the length of my right forearm and lashed a one in a half inch chain around it and then the other half of the chain to a pick axe I found in the gardening section. Just so the pick axe met my needs I hacked a few screwdrivers in half and soldered them to the top of the pick axe and added a nice hacksaw blade to the brim of it so that there was enough weight to establish damage if I were to throw it.

I prepared my body for internal and external injuries. I numbed the very essence of my soul, the black hole now dwells. There's a light twitch that is stress induced that plagues my right eyelid. It is nothing major but serves as a reminder for a few moments until I set off on my journey, I'll get to remember my true nature is hiding.

I am ready.

There is a zest of moisture collecting across the handle of the pick axe as the hollow shell of Blink stood in the pupil of the store's exit. In his right hand the axe in his left hand Theodore's head held waist high by the hair follicles. A steaming cloud of grief encircled Blink and his carried head. Blink's eyelids wafted over his eyeballs creating darkness. His wallowing breathes stiffened stifling the sound.

The exterior of the store had hundreds of vehicles structured in a placement for tactical cover along elongated paved white lines. Sifting through the air was a harmonic noise of frantic tapping. This nostalgic and ominous sound delivered threats of the endeavors soon to pass. The night demanded obedience from the citizens inside its web. Not a soul stirred. The barren city sidewalk outside the store lopped up the garbage and freedom before the stepped on upcoming hours. Porous the peace and tranquility hiccupped tithes of malcontent. The white lines stretched in an "E" shape facing downward.

Mildew famished the trash breathing down the street. Every stitch of bacteria combing the garbage wafted feverishly into the air trying to gain the upper hand on the world. Fertile ropes of light perched on selective glossy surfaces so that the road of unseen danger stayed fulfilled and content.

"Where to first?" Blink lashed his words out grappling for an answer with haste.

"Across the lot." The glassy pin like eyes of his pierced up at Blink.

Blink answered with a quick jolt of his body towards the center white line of the "E". As his weight was added to the lot the floor bowed underneath him and tar like clutched to his feet. With a desperate conviction of confusion he swung the pickaxe through the nearest vehicles window latching on to the frame of the door. With his upper body Blink pried his feet from the substance across the lot and climbed on top of the vehicle void of paint.

"What just happened?" Blink vomited anger into Theodore's face.

"Careful." Theodore grinned wide as his eyebrows raised.

The cars at the other end of the "E" structure began to roll down the now apparent slope caused by Blink's added weight to the lot. One bland vehicle complied with rust rolled towards Blink's occupied position. Blink swung his neck to the left as he noticed other vehicles sliding towards his position. Blink leapt into the air stinging the scene with a stench of escape. Blink landed on a new vehicle coated in a sky blue haze of paint shavings. The metallic hunk of blue glitter shrieked.

"Oh, set off an alarm. This is going to be fun." Theodore belted Blink in the face with his realization.

From across the lot staggered out three individuals from an overturned semi truck's trailer. One of the three that exited had a leather hood skin tight draped over his head and two slits in the face for its eyes to peer out. This being also wore a skin tight arrangement of chains and spikes lining the upper body and wore shorts matching the rest of his gear but he wore knee high boots with claws jetting out the sides and bottom of it. The second creature to leave the trailer was a five foot gremlin type beast that had two arms covered in gadgetry and it only had four teeth that resided on the upper mandible. The third wore a crash test dummy scalp for a hat and had a respirator hooked up to its mouth as it held the canister lashed to its back.

The gremlin chomped his teeth into his right forearm turning on some kind of gizmo as the respirator beast climbed into its own amateur looking welded on armor plated vehicle. The skin tight creature bounded on top of a car and added weight to the ground bowing it as vehicles began to roll sporadically. The gremlin used his arms to control the bowing manually instead of the initial weight activation.

Blink slammed Theodore's neck cavity into a hood ornament and sailed his way into the air aiming for another vehicle that had started to roll off towards the oncoming skin tight creature. The creature's car rolled towards Blink's with a steady pace. Blink reared back and tossed the pickaxe towards the creatures center torso. It curled its self backwards bending limbo style out of the way of the weapon as it used its skillful reflexes to leech its poisonous grasp on the chain links attached to the pickaxe, and it tugged Blink forward off balance making him stumble off his vehicle. He crashed directly into the front of the creatures vehicle holding his chain. Recuperating instantly and with a sudden tuck inward of his legs, the vehicle collided with his previously occupied vehicle. The front bumper rocketed against the engine and collapsing the hood as Blink lay atop of it.

With a quick lash out of furry Blink connected the pickaxe to the creature's shin splitting what bone he had in two. The faucet of blistering fumes exited the beast's vocal chords as Blink raised to his feet but quickly they were swept from his possession because the vehicle occupying monster crashed directly into the rear driver's side door. Blink's weight dented the hood as pain shocked his hip bone. A slight of hand maneuver brought a specially formed cocktail into view.

The creature with the split shin clutched his injury with all its might as its malicious hate roared from its lungs into Blink's face. Blink returned the hatred and disbanded the contents of the bottle into the face of the beast as it cowered in a compilation of extreme pain flares. A secondary strike found its way into the neck of the creature as Blink pierced its left jugular with the pickaxe, an applause of blood and plasma joined the scene.

Blink pounced towards the retreating vehicle occupied by the other beast whom chose to attack Blink. The chain attached to his wrist and the pickaxe which was still lodged in the other creature's throat cavity. Blink knelt on the hood with a booming hello from his landing as he pinched his left finger tips into the bridge between both hood and windshield. The chain tightened dragging the climbing monster off its vehicle and down into the absorbing gravel. Blink smiled at the creature which seeing Blink's amusement enraged him completely as he punched the gas trying to accelerate to a deadening speed. Blink prepared himself as they came over the previous creature, Blink used the vehicle's bumper grinding on the chain from the stress placed on it to cause a spark which ignited the liquid rallying across the gravel rotting creature.

A sudden halt of the metal can of a machine crumpled under the weight of the impacted object of the same mass. Blink rocketed forward into the windshield of another machine. The burning body of the first beast of mayhem drug right underneath the gas tank of the vehicle which from long rusting had a hole dripping fuel. With these series of unfortunate events the vehicle erupted into thousands of shrapnel pieces striking out at any object in the vicinity. Blink was struck by a dime sized aluminum railing in the gut. It intruded in on the epidermis sailing blood down the backs of many condemned emotions.

Blink's chain rigging was no more as the ground below his new platform sunk. All the mindless metallic beasts proceeded to Blink's position at a grueling pace. Blink rhythmically pulled his body from its glass shattered cradle and he paraded across two vehicles so he could scoop up Theodore's head. Theodore pulsed his eyelids as Blink tore Theodore from his hood ornament stature and up into a protective fortified wall of caring. Theodore peeled the placid tint from his emotions and bounced around a chance of maybe letting a piece of his interior out for this Blink character.

With every bound from metallic beast to metallic beast of Blink's, Theodore tied his thoughts into bundles of congealed rations of information for use. He prepared his knot of friendship so that access could be granted if sought, he also aligned retaliation and survival knots. A rustic hood crumpled under the weight of Blink while Theodore poured acid into his thoughts, readying to destroy any chance any outside force could have of obtaining them. His uneasy rapture came from his untrusting nature of anything not his own species.

I finished this attack off in a swift but forceful manner. I butchered this creature as it cowered crying for an idol I could not recognize. I refuse to recognize. I think it talked about its lord. But here I can not help think as its blood squeals from my fingertips and onto its ripped open facial cavity. Its now a black hole of torn flesh shielding what darkness is beneath, but it called out for a higher presence. Was it God? Did it call out to my Lord? If that's so then how do I know that they are not blessed and suppose to overtake the world I know as I die, in the corner crying HIS name. The blood of my victims have stained my finger nails. I've placed my whole body into a damned basket ready to be checked out and sentenced into a fiery prison.

I feel a weary presence overtake my limbs as I plop a seat next to this faceless creature to my right, the darkness of the trailer blankets both of us. I speak of course about me and Theodore. Maybe, I say this loosely, but maybe I feel a pinch of longing for conversation. Just an object that can hear my words and respond in a verbal manner so that I don't writhe into a convulsing carcass of oblivion. A friend, no, my friends have all become stains on the concrete below.

I'm infected by my own genetics, the human race.

"So boss, you like the unsatisfying kind more eh?" The sarcasm blistered Blink's eardrums as Theodore bumbled around in Blink's right palm.

"What happened to your 50's lingo?" Blink retaliated as he pushed a needless conversational piece into the mold.

"Sorry boss thought you'd like me to try something more in your time period. What would you say that is? Hmm maybe mid nineties?" Theodore grazed the rotting flesh next to his ear with his eyes as he smoldered in content.

"That was seventy years ago. Well beyond my time. We don't live as long as your kind." Blink sanded down the peace between the two conversing bodies.

"Yeah, well I guess if your neighbors annoying you there is not need to kill him then, just wait him out. Hell we could have done that!" Theodore joked as his eyebrows arched. "Why do you do this?"

A clean sweep of corrosive numb drained Blink's mind. "I... guess its because ... I'm the only one to do it."

With haste Theodore answered bluntly, "That's not an answer. Why do you do this?"

A banished gaze bore out of Blink's eyes and into the far trailer doors. A silence scratched the room with a screech. "I don't remember. Any feelings I've had before this meaningless romp. This mission I've been sent on is the last real memory that I can cling to, but there must have been a reason. I remember my childhood vaguely, I remember my life as if I were looking through a dense fog. I see the Bible clearly though. Funny isn't it. Something I actually have no real passion for coming up and gripping my mind only. I think there's a reason for that. I hope there is a reason for that. Maybe there's a reason for everything. For this I keep going. This is the only reason I know."

Theodore winked with monetary muscle spasms of laughter, "God? Yeah, sure. I heard about the guy."

Blink latched his pupils on the door handle to exit the trailer. His voice ripped a solemn guiltless reverberation from his diaphragm "The fool has said in his heart, "There is no God." They are corrupt, they have done abominable works, there is none who does good… God said that."

The trailer vibrated abruptly knocking the faceless creature over till it pinned Theodore his side settled position. Jetting in from both sides of the trailer were violent swarms of song filled musk reeking the melody of anger and scorn. Swift and malicious laughter accompanied the musk as it harmonized causing a dreary emotion to overcome Blink. Blink froze, thorns.

"My nightmare comes."

PARADE

"Lets play a game."

"Lets play a game."
"Lets play a game."

    The entire trailer begun to turn ninety degrees to the right as a clean grinding silhouette cascaded from the street below. Theodore lopped up the poison of worry. Blink was the dignitary of paralysis as his face continued its fear stricken countenance. The neighboring soulless body laughed wildly from its torn facial cavity. From the trailer's only access point came a hand intruding the space occupied by Blink, the hand carried a pink teddy bear.
    The teddy bear was placed by the dilapidated hand on the trailer's floor. The hand wiggled the bear about acting like it was talking as a high pitched voice erupted through the compartment in a mocking demeanor, "Hey there Blink, we came to play a game. LETS PLAY A GAME!"
    "Lets play a game."

"Lets play a game."
"Lets play a game."

The trailer doors opened revealing hundreds of heads on sticks with only smiles, the sticks were the bodies of the heads, they moved and bounced around as they twittered to one another. Pronounced in a menacing stance stood the nightmare in the center. He wore nothing but a brown bag over his head with a painted on smiling face, the rest of his body has digressed from the costume and his skin was carved into "V's" and burned for the glossy flesh appeal. His hands were extended as he offered a revelation to Blink's eyes.

The paper bag jittered back and forth as the nightmare pounced his words into the trailer, "Funny how we meet. Like my painting? I think I'd call myself a dilettante wouldn't you? I dabble in and out of art forms. Do you want to see another? I've got a great artsy game for us. For us all, Theodore. You wouldn't honestly think I would over look you too. No, my games are for everyone, and every kind."

Theodore's mouth wobbled about in a diffident sputter, "How? How do you know me?"

Prancing from side to side the stick heads added a chorus of laughter to the sea of confusion. "Ah, your head's at a loss Blink. Theodore I don't think you completely understand what I am. Hell neither does Blink over here. I am the coagulation of all your lost dreams, but I turn them to hate one another and join into one, a nightmare. So, lets get this game a started shall we!"

"Lets play a game. Lets play a game, lets play a game." The heads spoke in unison as they staggered themselves into a single file line. "Lets play a game."

Marching out from behind a long drawn out stage covered in blood and fecal matter was an odd assortment of adults and teenagers, all dressed up in their Sunday best. The sticks lined up on the opposing side of the stage all bubbly and fused with excitement.

The nightmare clung his right arm onto the trailer door and peered on in to direct his words to Blink, "The rules are simple, each stick died in a certain odd manner. That means the others have to try to figure out how the sticks did it, simplicity is the key." While the nightmare spoke he added a slight swinging gesture to his posture to absorb all the anxiety from the hovel of Blink's. The air wept as the game begun.

"BEGIN."

A dark haired woman tapped her feet up and onto the stage getting her high heeled shoes dabbled in pieces of coagulated blood. Her hair tussled itself all over her head as she swiped it back and out of the way. She smiled delighted and enthusiastic, "My name is Thelma and I am going to be trying to figure out Jack the stick's death."

An eager applause erupted from both sides of the stage, the human beings clapped, the sticks chirped. The nightmare cocked his head inward to Blink's stationary placement. The painted on smile egging Blink on but he could not move.

Jack the stick galloped its deformed body on stage nodding happily as Thelma looked Jack over. Her eyes seemed to glide over his stick body with an ease of hopelessness. "I guess this wont work." She looked away and pondered to herself. "If I were named Jack and I wanted to kill myself how would I do it." A light bulb imminently kicked on in her head. "I've got it. Can a stick please?"

The nightmare continued to stare into the trailer, "I think she's got this one."

Thelma slowly and surely took off both high heeled shoes and then covering her entire backside with blood she sat down on the stage. "Well I think Jack was a cross dresser, so if I were him. Well, here if I were going to kill myself I would first open up the flesh right under my chin and connecting to my throat. Then using the stick I'd thrust it up through, but first need to open it with the high heels. Oh, I'm not good at explaining things, let me show you. "

A slight panic smile reverberated from her face as she propped the heel up to the bridge of her lower jaw. She inhaled the salted emotions and want from the tainted air. With a teeth grinding thrust upward she impaled the lower jaw right below the chin next to her neck with her right shoe's heel. Her eyes rolled upward cowering in pain as her fingertips flicked about angrily convulsing. The other heel was next.

The two heels clapped as she drove it into her throat beside the twin shoe. Bowing her head over she pinned the shoes against her chest while with exasperated screams from her nasal passages she pressed with both hands on the toes of the shoes and pried open a clean red waterfall entry way into her innards. Blood bathed her like a mother would her child, peace ravaged her body. She was dying, but needed to complete the game. With a twist of determination she scratched her fingernails against the stick and then in one zealous movement her entire consciousness warped into death. Her fingers reached trying to escape the body as her legs tried to run away from the horror, but her cheeks smiled enjoying every bit.

The nightmare raised his hands approving her attempt, "Ladies and gentlemen we have a match! Jack in fact did kill himself cause he was a cross dressing homosexual. He did in all reality use his gay heels to murder himself! Give a round of applause for Thelma!" The uproar of cheers pulsed through the air and into Blink's veins. The nightmare spilled his love of the game into the trailer by gazing right back at Blink and Theodore in a mischievous nature.

"Lets play a game, lets play a game, lets play a game."

Blink wrestled with the friable freight of his own eulogy, "I did nothing." Beside Blink the dead carcass turned frolicking the steam of its own loathing musk across the noses of Theodore and Blink. The condemning frill upon Blink's nose stung as it attacked his morals, body, spirit. The sounds of the game continued to be mishandled by Blink's eardrum and caused the body to lament the audible sense.

"My name is Byron, I will be trying to figure out what Lora the stick did to … kill herself." Byron wore a bright green tie with a nicely ironed tuxedo. His appearance offered the joyous crowd a hearty mirthful uproar of laughter. "Ah, I got it. Maybe she slammed her face in some knives. Bring me knives." Carried to the stage was device with four knives propped up by three metal bracers set out in a triangle fashion. Two children dressed formally as if prepared for a wedding set the device down for Byron's disposal. Byron became shaky and questionable as his nerves begged him not to follow through. Byron managed to over throw his worry for a moment as he bashed his face into the pointed objects brought for his show. A groaning feverish wailing erupted from Byron. "IT hurts! Why! MY GOD!" Byron had pierced his left eyeball, right brow, upper right cheekbone, and his left inner ear canal through his far left cheek.

Instantly from Byron's mistake the nightmare bounded onto the stage splashing blood into the crowd and accompanying the new waves of red in Byron's face. Byron was on his side laying there trembling as he screamed and vomited at the same time. "Get the hell off my stage." The nightmare growled with maliciousness.

Byron's lips drooled the inner acid of his stomach while perching the draining blood from his face, "But I did what you told me… I played the game."

The nightmare's arms twitched in aftershocks to obfuscate what image there was of himself. "You failed the game. You will have to live, but in pain."

Byron's body convulsed in a salacious leap to his feet. He paraded about laughing and gliding through the blood coating the floor. The knives still inhibiting his facial structure as his facial movements sliced more flesh and muscle from his identity. "I played your game I played your game. Didn't I. I played your game." Both the ulna and the radius in both left and right arms split in two dangling still attached but never able to be reconnected. Byron wailed as he urinated on himself and tried to vomit again but nothing exited.

The nightmare kicked the blood from his feet onto the crowd as they watched Byron in silence. "You will survive and become a monster in your society, people will hate you. Your friends will not be able to stand looking at you. You will wish for death but not be able to get to it. This is my doing. Remember that, you've upset me. This game is over."

There is nothing left of his presence, a ghost of fallen souls. My mind stained with their screams and cries, while condemned with the bruise of not helping. They enjoyed it all. How do I believe I can over come this? Something like that nightmare is impossible to diminish in any way. The crowd in my inner sanctum has all gone home, there is nothing backing me in my corner. I couldn't move. That is the only thoughts bludgeoning my vocal chords, "SCREAM IT OUT, TELL SOMEONE BLINK!" I couldn't move. What passive chance could a timid scavenger of the barren mindless wastelands have against the uprising heartless force I named my nightmare.

A blanket of shock trimmed any and all egotistical emotions from Theodore's head, "What did I just see? That was not one of us."

I polished the stone of realization for my fellow head, "Yes, he was real. You are the first being I've had the privilege to share his company with. Nice guy isn't he."

Squinting Theodore faced a prism of enlightenment, "I believe I've just seen the devil."

I squandered out a primal quirked smiling gesture, "Nothing short of. The demon that haunts me. But I can do nothing when he's around, something in the air that controls my body. I call it thorns."

Sniffing the air as if trying to pull back time Theodore gazed up at me, "Why don't I help you get rid of this thing. Forget the mission of ending us all for a bit. What if we just set out to destroy this nightmare first? It will save us all some trouble, on both sides."

Humans, the living embodiment inflation of the world's greed. Man, are we more apelike, pithecoid or are apes more humanistic, anthropoid? Plesiadapis to Smilodectes to Pilopithecus to Proconsul to Oreopithecus … where in this evolutionary chain have we learned to breed morals? Is this infestation I baste in anything more then a conjured up flavor from cooks of the Neanderthal Epoch? Did we comb this from a lesser then equivalent species? There is a labyrinth of stimuli lurking in my humanoid spectrum. I am a result to stimulus' of every kind, blocking out nothing., but this changes due to the event at hand. In all animals if threatened turn off certain needed senses in order to amplify others. There is a stimulus here I must tickle of this nightmare that follows me about. If I could solve its wants and needs I could manipulate them and catch this thing off guard and maybe lure it into a trap.

Pistons of emotions fire off obvious answers to my dilemma but refuse to blossom true accomplished satisfaction. Flaws of each answer picnic across my scorched imagination that I arise into failure almost at will. I browse the files of my brain for a remote answer that has probably been buried or erased. Saliva paints the roof of my mouth with acidic frustration. I don't know.

I pried at Theodore's bargain, "You don't know what it is, neither do I. What could possibly be done on either end to stop such a thing. You've seen what it can do, and still you believe there is a way to stop it. Or kill it in that matter."

Theodore grinned immensely causing his little body of a head to stretch oddly, "I believe so, but first we need your guns. I will tell you how to find them, no more deception. We are on a mission."

He told me about his deception, his knowledge about the parking lot assault. His verbal mapping of my friends whom were held captive led a trail directly backtracking to an individual whom I trusted. The Stuttering Prophet. Little has he helped me since my digression of abstract thought, but he was around. Well I think he was. The frigid winter of my cleansed palette diminishes my analytical skills to an almost childlike demeanor. I've caused my head to swell with ammonia like properties, toxic, oxygen consuming, inflammation and burning. Wait, ammonia. Oxygen loss adds to muscle impairment and tunnel vision. Ammonia, could it be the culprit. Magnetism causes blisters of light to form across the images received just like pressing against the pupil. Could there be a link between all of these components? Slowly I will unravel the mystery of my nightmare.

I will meet my prophet and he will accompany me and my friends, Amy and Sty to the wall of woes, his own creation.

REVERSE REPO

Human tissue preservation is simplistic in all aspects, remove and freeze for later usage. New chemicals have been applied to this commonly repossessed organ for a newly diverse array of uses. Formaldehyde based solutions have been introduced to the chemical bonds introduced into these tissue cells to help preserve them along with a mixture of 4 percent of sodium nitrite, and 6 percent of hypo chlorite. Formaldehyde alone is used to fix tissue in post mortem bodies set for embalming. In some places in this society human tissue is passed about like currency. One of these factories for removing and distributing this currency is where I found my deceptive friend The Stuttering Prophet.

I've become acquainted with this head of mine, I declare ownership of him. He's become quite helpful in directing my passage through the infested highways of hell I refer to as my city. The nightmares lurking on each street corner and in the eyelash of every road sign has been avoided, this has been a delightful change of pace. The rhythmic clatter of my feet progress my flesh built vessel into a worm hole of concrete paved ally ways and to my finish line carved in coagulated blood extract and preservatives.

The night continued, time has passed enough for day but still the sun has not breached the night's gates. "Where are we?"

Theodore rolled his facial muscles around to initialize conversation as the surrounding dark alleyway setting peel itself away and revealed a road of bodies lying on their backs as they wept into the spiraling purple clouds above, a violet hue furbished the surroundings. "Never land… pfft… fuck if I know." Theodore's eyes followed the pileus layer capping the cumulus as the cumulus rotated through the pileus layer creating a skirt of condensation and moisture.

The black hole above absorbed the woes of the road ahead as pain condensed into a liquid and escaped willingly out through each porous carcass. The blossomed incarnation of pain liquid became buoyant in the midst of the cloud's rotation. It danced in the core while a barrage of dulcet and tranquil music ravaged and internalized its zest into each listening spirit.

I reached out uttering a conversational piece with my touch sense through the nerves in my fingertips. The air did not feel any different and the image folded into a two dimensional image as my hand touched the sedimentary exterior of a building's wall. The bodies evaporated and so did the violet hue contaminated clouds, all that was left was a chipped brick wall stretching the length of the alleyway and up eight stories.

Theodore hand fed laughter into the night air, "We saw a mirage, they are common around the Repo building. It is caused by the noxious fumes escaping the corpses as they decompose. I've never seen it though until now. Fucks with ya a bit don't it.

I proceed to intake oxygen as my vocal chords retaliate to the image I consumed, "I don't understand your change in tone and diction. But is this the place?"

Theodore smiled with anticipation, "Yes, it is. Are you going to paint the walls with their blood?"

My eyes shut, "This conversation is dilatory in nature."

Theodore jitters about excitedly beneath my right underarm, "Your tongue just adds to the anxiety of a massacre. Give me the details after your through, every blood spilling detail."

I laid Theodore down beside a crippled brick at the corner of the wall, "I'll find a stapler for you."

Theodore watched me check around the corner to scope out the front of the building, "Why?"

I ran my eyes down a building stained with importance, there was no damage nor even a strand of barbed wire guarding the entrance. It stood inviting, luring. It contained a layer of mirrors all redirecting the sights on another individual instead of on it and its inhabitants.

I glanced back at Theodore in a smirk, "For your mouth if you don't shut up."

A flash of color sparked in my eyes. Nothing.

I felt myself breathing.
I continued to live.
Darkness befriended my sight.
Everything was over, or it should have been.

I blinked as my eyes shuttered from the abrupt attack from the florescent light above of the street lamp. It was then when I heard the voice grazing on my eardrums it was that of a creature whom knew my friend, Theodore.

A growl mixed voice pinched the lobes of Theodore's ear, "I save you Theo. You are in danger and I save you."

An exhausted exhale from Theodore's little remaining respiratory system sparked agitation into the new being, "Thank you Neecro but I was not in danger. This is not a human but a converted."

I flicked my vision towards this new interacting object occupying space beside Theodore. It, Neecro, stood roughly seven feet tall with a burly structure, his upper torso resembled that of a cloche because of its bell shape stature. Its pigment bore frost like characteristics while in total contrast to its eyes which pulsed red to yellow with its breathing. I banished air from my lungs warning Theodore of my conscious status.

Prickly and alert Theodore tapped a dance with his lower mandible as he laced words into Neecro's mind, "Oh, let me introduce the one you bludgeoned. Blink. He is a converter. And there were these rogues whom snatched his weapons and hid them in the Repo building."

Neecro snarled with a gust of animalistic rage, "I hate the Repo building. They don't care about their own. They just repo everything."

I prodded my tongue around my gums as I lopped up the remnants of any blood so I could extract them from my body, "Neecro, I believe this is your name. If you help me for just a moment I could then forget about what you did to me and everyone will be a bit happier. Or we can work this out and you become a nice little monument right in front of this building you love so much."

A popped blister of malicious content scarred the area with a dull silence, until Theodore chipped it away. "I would just let that one go Neecro, you did just knock the hell out of him."

All the chords of mine snapped as I locked in on this creature's glare towards me. It laughed in my direction. The next impulse of mine, raise up, became intertwined with the removal of the last Molotov cocktail. I blinked using muscle memory for my actions. Eyes opened revealing the glimmer of glass fluttering about into the night sky while this new fellow's nose split in two down the left nasal passage. The removal of mass added to the simplicity of hiding the dangerous piercing ends of the glass into an eye socket of its, while it still recuperated from the initial strike. A clockwise twist removed all thoughts of "pain could be present" and transformed it to intense crippling agony.

I transferred my gaze down to Theodore, "You started all of this."

Theodore wrapped a smile across his cheeks, "I know."

I positioned my body up against the wall improving myself a way into the building. "Let him know."

Theodore flashed his eyes at Neecro and commanded obedience, "Strike ahead of you, that's where he is."

The master and follower route progressed nicely as Neecro lunged his entire body forward trying to catch the artist whom created a masterpiece on his canvas. I tossed my quick witted plan into action with my sudden dodge of Neecro. Neecro's body mass and force were enough to erupt the wall away from the foundation completely. Neecro's presence inside the Repo facility loomed as an oddity as no sound passed in or out of the imploded wall.

A surprise echoed from my facial expression as I acknowledged my friend, "Good work."

With hesitation on a string I entered the hole.

The noxious gasses expelled from the decay of past human being's thoughts remained in a noose of ferocious cravings, life, happiness, and love. The skin moldings of human beings dangled above the floor suspended by hooks impaling their foreheads. Across the floor were rolled up human skin but the neck and head remained unrolled and propped up by foot tall cylinder pegs checkered across the floor. Everything remained motionless and waiting.

Blink noticed all the human remains were burdened with magnetically opposing forces repelling the unsatisfied death of their but enjoying the presence of the new able body. Each bag of flesh had been cleverly placed in positions of an audience to bear witness to Blink's arrival.

In an unsynchronized musical tone a voice bounced around the building, "Y…yoou…ooo actually came to th…this place… Blink?" In unison but a beat behind the speaker all the boneless skin bodies mimicked the voice with their own wails and moans. *(Came to this place)* "I…I actually felt some h. heart ache when… nnn…. I was telling … you … ooo to leave to oo your death." *(Leave to ooo your death)*

Blink wrangled up a meaningless retort, "When did you start enjoying music, Stuttering Prophet?"

Without a word from the Stuttering Prophet came the musically moaning solo of the soulless flesh, *"Cry for me Blink, so the river can run high. I do not enjoy music but the sound of men who die. You proceeded to end all my fears, ever since we've known each other, these ever so long years."*

Blink encouraged the stress level of his to remain mild but it churned higher and higher with every syllable sung my the choir of dead. Behind Blink Neecro shook and trembled whining in pain. Blink's arms sprouted goose bumps as destruction erected itself inside his heart. "Afraid to reveal yourself Prophet?"

Hot acidic moisture built up across the unwelcoming room as the Stuttering Prophet bellowed from an unseen location, "Y…your powerless witho… out your weapons Blink. How…how can you … ou … even think to… ooo come in… in here with ou… out a weap … on?"

Blink stepped forward next to a drape of flesh as Neecro erected himself fully for a brutal assault, "I wouldn't say I'm completely weaponless."

Blink sidestepped to the left directly evading Neecro's flailing attack while Neecro's fist soared through the skin drape and ripped it in two as prolonged screams jetted out from its pores. Neecro became covered in flesh particles full of hatred and agony. The head of the skin drape acted as if it had teeth and proceeded to gnaw on Neecro's neck with its lips.

Blink peeled his lips back in a smile, "You see I've got myself a bull, now just give me what I came here for."

Startling Blink The Stuttering Prophet's voice shrieked out from beside him as Blink watched the prophet's face pressed tightly against the skin of a woman's stomach, "Funny how… how humans are. Nothing m…more then handbags.," He tore his face from her abdomen and poked his head around the flesh so he could rest his stare on the creature he had built, Blink. "Do… do you…ooo even know why you are here? Is…is it just for y… your t…two weapons, or d…d…do yoou feel a lo…nging to be with something? Do …do you want a com… companion? That's wh… why it hurt you … ou so much to real …realize I had been…been manipu…lating you all th…through your tor…tor …tormented occupation."

Blink cocked his head to the left spraining his muscles with a prolonged smile, "God is a just judge, and God is angry with the wicked every day. If he does not turn back, He will sharpen His sword; He bends His bow and makes it ready. He also prepares Himself instruments of death; He makes His arrows into fiery shafts. His majesty has prepared me, His instrument of death, and it is bearing down at you right now Prophet. Take this warning, be weary on how you proceed."

The Stuttering Prophet filtered out all his emotions in one single blink, "You have no idea do you…" His eyes flickered back and forth from one hanging satchel of flesh to another. "Y…you will have a… a fun time in … in the oo … old town tonight… fire …fire…"

Directly following the last words of The Stuttering Prophet the impaled bodies slid down ripping their flesh in two as they slopped against the cold absorbed floor below. With each rag like slop to the floor each entity laughed hysterically by the lower extremities fluctuating so that there could be a vacuum caused to act as lungs. Two massive piles of smoldering flesh plummeted towards Blink as he dove forward escaping the attack. Decaying flesh sprayed across the prize of the night, Blink.

Blink slammed his eyelashes shut concealing his delicate pupils to the foreign objects at hand. His eyes trimmed the darkness away as they opened revealing to Blink's surprise all the cases of human remains crawling and clawing their way to his position. Blink

Blink raised up completely as he prepared for an attack but the closest body became liquid and splashed itself across Blink's epidermis. An acidic erosion started taking place across his visible skin, his break submerged in the signals of pain erupting from his outer layer. A vocal chord ripping shriek bleated from Blink's inner sanctum as he dropped to his knees quaking.

The Stuttering Prophet watched in excitement as the rest of the flesh rags gathered around him basking in the torment of the enemy. The ripe shrills from The Stuttering Prophet's foe lashed out at all whom stood by praying upon his weakness. The prophet's hands tickled their way up into the reverberation of pain and danced about adding humility to the stew of emotion.

Neecro grinded his teeth as he approached Blink's feeble status. Neecro's body steamed from the acidic wear and tear on his flesh but nothing mattered but to injure the entity known as Blink. Neecro occupied the withering musk to the left of Blink, a pulsing grimace forced itself into Neecro's muscles. Neecro spread his arms to both sides locked and loaded for his first impact into Blink territory.

Blink raised up with blurring speed as he dug a metallic pin from his belt deep into Neecro's neck and immediately thrashed his index and middle fingers up into his neck cavity. With a ferocious tear Blink removed the forefront flesh of Neecro's neck creating a free fall of blood to cascade down. Blink quickly cupped his palms together and caught the liquid and bathed his skin in it and facial tissue to remove the acidic material. The basic nature of the blood at about 7.0 ph level to 7.8 counter acts the acidic properties of the foreign liquid.

Blink turned towards The Stuttering Prophet during the beginning stage of drainage from the most outer layer of blood coating his extremities. Blink's hands pried deep into Neecro's flesh as Neecro capped off his neck with his teetering hands. Blink removed two large leathery pieces of pale skin from Neecro as he then proceeded towards The Stuttering Prophet with a flaming vigor.

A large mass consuming towel of flesh threw itself towards Blink but with his new Neecro skin coating Blink's hands could catch the flesh and continued on his path. Still holding the flesh Blink used his other hand to block another assault of flesh, now he held two large flesh masses in each hand. Blink arrived feet from The Stuttering Prophet as the prophet reached out and burrowed his claws into Blink's chest. Blink refused to flinch as he clapped both bodies against the prophet's cheeks and pulled the prophet closer.

As Blink returned words for strikes saliva pasted to The Stuttering Prophet's face, "You will follow my lead, my friend."

Blink compressed his body low to the floor as the prophet kept his stance. Blink thrashed about gathering each bag of flesh for the prophet's gain. Blink wrapped The Stuttering Prophet with all the skin fragments of once occupied souls. Pleasure developed instantly while screams surged from The Stuttering Prophet.

Bound up the prophet found security in his only means of conveyance of his pain, screams. He fumbled around with his saliva draining into his throat as coughs erupted allowing him to view his flesh flicking from his body with each contraction of his lungs. The vision etched into his sight was that of Blink grinning with ecstasy as the sins of his devoured him from the outside in. The prophet shut his eyes in a blink of dry impulse and concern, when opened he gazed upon an unfamiliar sight. Sty's eye's gleamed inches from The Stuttering Prophet's.

"You blinked."

Sty and Amy greeted their companion with a hearty sliver of heat and steam of gunpowder. Blink reversed the offered love and applied some of his own by cleaning the blood and flesh from Sty. Blink's lips curled above his teeth. "We sure do make a mess now don't we. Let's go pay a visit to our nightmare."

Absolute Threshold.

My eyes complete the accommodation process as the ciliary muscle changes the thickness of the lens so my vision can now focus on my returned friends. The neural responses converted from light in the photoreceptors tell me, nothing is wrong, but I feel something radiating from Sty's handle. I fear there might just be a problem with my retinal disparity, the displacement between the horizontal positions of my gun's corresponding image in both eyes. The process of information within my visual cortex lingers in a standby status as I compute the plan at hand.

Three attackers and a head will try to destroy a being that even sends fear into "Them". My damaged reflexes might not be able to recognize the nightmare. I object taking on something I just can not find a weakness to, but I believe I've stumbled upon the magical illusion. Well in all actuality I have only figured out a few of its tricks and methods.

I rest on a step up towards the atrium of mutilation as Theodore sways, impaled on a hook once used to hold up dormant flesh. Theodore's tongue encircled his lips as saliva and joyous extracts sputtered from his enjoyment. His chin pranced back and forth dancing with his shadow as they choreographed a unique frolic of pleasure.

The building seemed to agree with Theodore's current status. The paint shavings and coagulated blood seamlessly smiled and nodded along to his tongue's rhythmic sloshing. The musk of death greeted me with arms outstretched. It pleaded for me to not proceed with my intentions.

Inside my skull a sizing of the stone structure I dwelt in currently begun to spiral around tossing up ideas of destruction. While my mind continued its over occupied calculations of the building my right hand checked the condition of Sty, and his ammunition. Full… who reloaded?

Instantly without warning a creature with chainsaw's for arms and a face and body covered in liquid latex. The flesh toned liquid latex caused a melted sunken look to the flesh. The creature erupted from beneath the stairs sawing the first four layers away in a matter of two quick breaths.

I under impulse raised my right hand not knowing a chainsaw accompanied the monster's attack as it pummeled Amy. Amy's metallic structure pried apart like a tin can under a torch. I spun around with a force of survival as I evaded the initial attack. The next shoulder bearing attack ended as I accompanied his right chainsaw towards a hook which caught it allowing me time to retrieve Sty. Sty reverberated his love into my palms as his barrel gazed deep into the chainsaw maniac's eyes.

The chainsaw maniac snarled as it whipped its head back mocking Sty and me. In a flash the creature raced to the right avoiding the meat hooks, its arms flailed about devoting a fireworks display of sparks behind it as a distraction. Light blotched out the creature's whereabouts as silence drenched the building. With the black burn of the light still lingering in my sight I pinched my eyelids and surveyed the territory trying to find my foe. My heart beat skipped as the attacker stood poised for an arms stretched upwards coming down the front of the victims face.

My reflexes declared dictatorship as I quickly twisted two chained hooks together in front of my body to offer protection. The chainsaw's bounced against the metallic chain links as sparks bedazzled the mid barrier between each clashing forces. My right leg carried with it my first intrusion of my enemy's boundaries. The shock of my kick corrupted the creature's stance and proceeded to drive the maniac backwards in an injured thrashing scream. The eighty percent human skin dust particles scathed the air like cockroaches a garbage heap. The maniac disappeared into the darkness looming behind his blanket of cover.

    Using Sty as a diversion I dropped him to my side while I used my other hand to reach cleverly behind me to grab a hold on the hook near my eye level. The lasso of sound roped the pursuer and delivered him racing his entire body and saws straight at my mid torso. I cocked my head to the left ducking just out of reach of the hook as I mobilized my entire upper body to drive the meat hook directly into the prefrontal cortex of the monster's brain. its burly arms teetered around its body as the rest of his carcass remained still. His arms danced about with the chainsaws still alive, the right chainsaw gingerly rocked into the right hand thigh, it removed eight inches of flesh and bone. Nothing happened with the beast. Everything was alright, not a single soul was harmed but its flesh resembled that of a meatloaf bathed in blood.

    "Over ambitious fool. I told him to wait for my command, then we all strike." The hissing howl of a woman's voice stretches across the skin of devastation. "But its all over now, our surprise would be less fulfilling."

    Quick flashes of light in strobe revealed a woman upside down without arms with her legs raised above her body and bowed over her sides keeping her mobile and her head from dragging across the ground. Her face was scabbed over from occasional points of contact with the paths created for feet. Her clothes continued to act as if she were right side up because they were stapled to her flesh.

    Darkness. A low rumble of hissing wafted through the opaque air like a toxic vapor. The strobe effect from an unknown light source ceased with a respite of light. "There are creatures here that would like to pay you a visit. We will do this … one by one…"

"One… by …one."

"One. By … one."

With corrosive intensity light erupted into sight. I squinted in convulsion as I watched a creature radiating the light. The creature's face was stretched facial tissue across a lampshade teetering on top of a 100 watt light bulb. The body was constructed with a thin gold inch wide metal tubing which formed the neck, the torso remained completely human as the arms and hands and feet were broken television sets acting as mouths chomping open and shut erratically. The arms formed a "T" as the televisions probed the surrounding area for viewers.

My right hand raised above the stifling beams of light piercing the darkness with razor blades. The facial tissue which was sprawled across the lampshade had its mouth widen as a groan flowed from an unseen location. The glass breaking screech of glass on metal insanely bludgeoned my eardrums.

I gently tapped the side of Sty preparing him for a textbook kill. "This is a threat?"

The flesh draped across the lampshade had its mouth fold inward and out as a voice bounded in stride, "I am merely an observer. I don't fight."

A fierce roar boomed adjacent my position as I wrapped my taste buds around the sight of a no armed, eight seven inch long fingers extruding from around a two foot gapping bite radius. The fingers scooped and carried the musk of the rotting corpses from the audience of oxygen. In a zest of overwhelming power each finger latched itself onto my face as an enormous suction started.

"Show you life and death in the form of humanity's definition."

In the image of an old mute film I watched the reel play out. I watched three men beating a man's face in with only the knuckles of their hands because their fingers had been removed with no surgical precision. A burn of light fogged up the reel causing the images of the three normal sized men to stretch and skew into fairytale villains. One lengthy villain reached down face to face with the victim who in the reel was unknown by a black cigarette burn in front of the person's face. White letters flashed up on the reel and read, "What do you have in the vehicle for us to kill you with." The next reel revealed in a corny fashion four objects; a screw driver, a pick axe, a crow bar, and a busted subwoofer. The woman screamed melodramatically as captions popped up saying "Scream". With eagerness steaming from their pores all three men grabbed a weapon of their choosing leaving behind the pick axe. The three had to use both sets of knuckles and palms to hold one weapon of theirs because of the lack of finger appendages.

    I sensed the mind of Sty as he directed my initial attack into the left thigh of the suction reel offering face placement sought creature. Within inches of prying my face from the erratic scratching and flailing of the fingers a face of an African American appeared from inside the mouth as its facial tissue began grading itself off and the fragments absorbed the floor's cool icy flavor of death. Featherlike each fragment floated questioning the direction it has chosen, but ultimately accepting its demise.

    The odd jumble of heel bounds alerted my senses as I turned to confront my new acquaintance. All that I could see was the upper half of a creature's face, a round gaunt nose structure and two light bulbs for eyes extruding the socket and on in full electric splendor. Momentary blindness kicked in as the dark burns shielded the outside world from my vision.

    Ratta tat tat. A low gargled hissing. The shuffling of antique novel's pages.

    A heavy groan from the left.

    An assertive whistle chanting from ahead.

    Silence.

    A clatter of erratic heartbeats together in almost unison to my right.

The metallic clang of an inch thick weapon.
Silence once again.

A clearing of phlegm from a set of raspy vocal chords bowled its way over the pins of silence.

The absent of pigment burn dwindled allowing the far left images to access my visual cortex. From the peripherals of mine I felt my courage corrode as a new creature leaned into view. This being had the misfortune of bearing two massive mouths where its eyes should be. "We can do this all day Blink. Surprised we know your name? I would be. You see I am not one but two beings occupying one mass. You … you're the same in a way. You are confused, torn in two for clashing ideas. I know this cause I can see into your soul. Yes, I have a gift. Like you … I can see the monsters inside. But you my man are in trouble. You are not here. This is a fantasy."

My eye sight eroded away as no vision was left. Everything remained in darkness. I could hear my heart beating… my breath squealing. I still lived. That was until my eyes opened.

"Blink… Blink… "My eyes blurred but adjusted to the image of a well dressed man in his mid fifties. "There you are… you dozed off there for a moment. Do you remember my last question Blink?"

My eyelashes clutched each other in bewilderment, "What… where am I… how do you know my name?"

The room had shielded itself from the outside by having a mellow beige color coating its surface. Directly hovering over me was a torture device gazing down at me clicking away as its chords. It spins the air towards me twisting the dew of peace into my hair follicles and scalp. The unknown man rested unenthusiastically behind a barren desk with two college ruled sheets of paper. My eyebrows bowed inward guessing and begging for answers all at the same time.

"I refer to you as Blink because that's what you have asked me to do… so, but that is not your name now is it … Blink? Do you remember your name? No… you cant. That is because your mind has a psychosomatic illness. In all basics your mind has a cold which needs to be rid of. Do you understand." The supposed doctor grinned a banana like in my general direction. Sparks sizzled within my skull.

My eyes twitched subduing my frustration with as little as possible. I wanted him to feel threatened, I wanted his lips to taste red lubrication as fear washes through his veins. "I've had the pleasure to have killed many a man whom has stood in my way. Now if you don't mind... let me go."

There pronounced in his forehead was an unflinching sign of confidence, "To what ... go kill monsters... that don't exist. You have been here for sometime. Lets be completely honest here...Blink... do you really believe you actually quested through a city of monsters and carried around a head that talked to you?"

Cascading through my nerves was a surge of anger and trivial questions, "This isn't real... they must have done something to me. This isn't real! What the fuck have they done to me!" I forged my way off the chair and onto my own two feet taking a stand in front of this man's happy go lucky life. The twilight of good morals peeked gingerly through the crevices of my lashes but the opposing spectrum lavished my behavior pattern. A tingling pinch fumbled across my back muscles as the questionable doctor's smile grew stretching over his face boundaries and past the width of the desk. It was about this time I became unconscious.

They had me stay within a room which they told me I've lived in for almost five years. This is a lie. The room had no wear or tear, no use came from its surfaces. I knowing what is inside this cerebellum of mine would have demolished every bit of peace radiating tint there was. That would have been the first week.

My nightmare, loosing my mind. Could the nightmare plaguing me conjure all of this? Maybe he is the doctor? Maybe he is in head of this place. Maybe I am crazy. Maybe.

I can faintly smell the gunpowder from Sty on my fingertips. This miniscule piece of evidence pointing to my knowledge of the past but then again it is still my word against his. My brain could be manipulating a common fragrance and turning it into something I want it to be. The mind is a powerful weapon to use against someone. Offer two suggestions of falsehood and doubt will set in, no matter how hard you believe. I can remember my ordeal in detail as my dreams rekindle the fire of past events. There have been some of "them" I have encountered that even I still don't believe happened.

They be stilled in me a schedule devised to transgress me into a mindless mobile piece of meat. But it wasn't until that moment of desperation and depravity in myself that I heard the voice. "Hey boss… Don't worry they don't know I'm here." The static buzzed through the speakers of the securely mounted television in each room of the building playing the same station. The television station sells antiques for high prices. This is all I know because during all this my attention focused itself elsewhere.

"Watch me, watch what you can never do. Unless you join me." The voice laughed in a galloping fashion all the way into my eardrums. The voice itself piloted out from the index finger of a unconscious man drooling on the bishop of a chess board game. The finger had teeth clapping together and raising apart with each syllable drifting from within.

My mouth bounded at the opportunity to confront my captor first hand, "It is you doing this isn't it? Your manifesting this damned psychiatric ward."

I believe I could see this finger smiling at me while it jabbered up and down, "You flatter me, but I wouldn't really imprison you now would I. I thought we knew each other that well, after all this time. You know you really shouldn't be talking to another man's finger. I don't think your doctor finds it quite healthy."

A jolt of abandonment expanded in my chest like a sponge, "Don't leave me here!" I impaled the man's finger with my fingertips trying to pry the mouth back open. The comatose man only vibrated slightly as security guards rushed around me to seize both my arms and subdue me from completing my mission.

The first guard cupped his left arm up under my right armpit thinking this flesh to flesh connection would not enrage my very core. I surprised him as I dug my fingers up under his jaw and into his neck squeezing the stylohyoid muscle in an immobilizing claws. His orchestra of muscles associated with the stylohyoid muscle all followed in tightening and swelling up. I then using a circular pattern swept the peace keeper off his feet and landed him safely in the realm of pain which was located between the shattering pieces of end table.

The civilian that failed to cling to my left arm had the beginning inch and a half of my middle and ring finger depart into the ventilation canals of his nostrils. Under my left hands mercy the security officer followed the slight twist of my wrist as his two arms met with my hand believing there could be a method out of my grasp. I answered his beliefs with a swift collapsible kick to the back of the knee causing the structure to dwindle in stance and in spirit. I agreed with the remaining inflation of pain to the man that his nasal passages will no longer be of interest as my right open palmed right hand struck the man in the tilted upward center of his forehead. Panic consumed the heart of the man so his mind shut down for safety purposes.

"Altruism, that's what this is. You have no consideration for your safety or anyone else's." The unnamed doctor declared his presence from the entry way lending a flush of disappointment and baffled stress to barrage all the objects within the room. "Obviously my client-centered therapy failed. What are you doing Blink?"

-What am I doing?
-Am I who I think I am?
-Did I really speak to a finger?
-Is this man right?
-Maybe I like this to much to stop?

My mouth made its way to the edge of the ice and froze while gazing down at the waterfall's height. I could not answer with a clear rationalization of my actions. I occupied the at fault station looming over the conditions of another obviously more over worthy employee "They" think that "We cant be seen ... then lets try you're the goose and lets yell out random obscenities." The commonality of this practice is a bore I still grow tired since by mind's clearance.

Sanity, would a definition be anything more then an everyday thought about how a certain human being performed in their life. How can this be sanity when we can not prove that this first leading being may or may have not been in their right mind. When did we decide that the normal mindset of individuals are what we believe it should be? We as a society have placed our fears and ideas in a hat and drew them out one by one taking other people's opinion on the matters instead of working on scientific fact. I compare my sanity with those of this sanitarium. I trust and believe no one. I doubt it all.

The doctor's damning glare parted the sea of humility as I obtained the realization of my legs pushing me towards his position. Stringing out the room stretched becoming elongated into a hallway, my legs actually continued to cooperate with my command node. The others within the room covered their eyes with unaware lenses.

The doctor fed himself a grin while my body sneered with every living tissue, "Seeing something Blink? It is called proximal stimulus, that is what you perceive optically in contrast to the actual physical world. What is it you see? Am I a monster? A creature or am I doing something impossible? Its all in your mind Blink. You are ill… why cant you believe that. Once you believe your in the real world with real people and not in this fantasy land you've created then you can start on your road to salvation, and become a civilized citizen of this community."

My knees quaked almost collapsing my foundation. Aftershocks follow my depression swelling in my cranial cavity. The pressure knots the pain around my earlobes and drags my head on a rope behind my body progressing over a road of nails. My right brow twitches, releasing the stress of the time elapsed beige purgatory. I figuratively feel my face melting from the bone and relieving my body of all the woe that has come from its countenance.

A fog of time blew away the world leaving a soul survivor, the image of myself as a child. I wore a purple shirt with green turtles in martial arts poses, also I had shorts made of jean material. I held a baseball cap in my right hand giving older self an absorbing blank stare. My child like appearance exhaled the freezing spores of failure. My lids became paralyzed while the innocent life nibbled upon my sojourn of sadness. With a blink my child image begun screaming at the top of its lungs as both of its legs splintered into pieces with flesh and blood pouring from each shin. Its arms attempted to desperately cling to the barren surroundings. No object was in its reach as fear popped its heart and feverish loathing hindered inside its prefrontal cortex.

This is me. All of this is in my mind. I am not sane. The pressure of everyday life must have fractured what little psyche there was to form an alternate reality for me to scurry into, to die in.

I witnessed in my right hand Sty form himself. It was almost like performing magic. This was the proof of my false reality. There in my right hand I held a gun, a weapon which came out of nowhere. Damning frustration rocketed through my right arm as my muscles conjoined with one last effort to disprove this doctor. The trigger was pulled. The boy's head, my childhood image, jettisoned off into all directions and particles. The echo of the gunshot waved farewell to such a childhood. The once real metal status of mine.

With hesitation but still proceeding, the darkness peeled away revealing a creature slumped to its knees with a wailing throat cavity connected to no head. The body became limp as blood flailed about overhead like a geyser of red syrup. A heartbeat bounded forth within my chest telling me I'm alive and awake.

With a thunderous shock a nine foot tall creature with wooden like stilt legs and four inch sunken eyes carried out a long glass axe with its burlap sack coved arms and torso. In a gallop the creature was directly ahead of me rearing back the axe for a downward attack. This position revealed an opening for an attack and I took it. I flexed my bicep for Sty to take aim at the creature's leg. Sty screamed focusing all his might on the creature's right wooden calf. The mid calf of the attacker splintered into fragments as all its force from the swing drug it down with it. My punishment for taking the leg out was not being able to move out of the way in time to save my body from the glass axe. The axe swooped low because of the leg malfunction and the tip to middle portion of the glass sliced through my upper left thigh. I witnessed my blood, in all their confusion, cling to the glass axe in desperation.

Pain flavored the room of hooks and darkness. My left leg gave way as tendons snapped, but I refused to fall. My right leg caught myself as I leaned over using Sty as a crutch. Blood poured from the crater in my thigh as the creature withdrew the axe and came in swiping from the side along the floor because of its newly acquired stance. The axe scraped along the floor roaring with each impact as I mustered the strength from my right leg to dive over the axe as it approached my feet. I thrashed my left hand outward to catch myself as my right hand clung to Sty, but this was a mistake. My left hand held up my left shoulder but allowed my lower mandible to collide with all my diving force into the concrete. I tasted a surge of saliva mixed red and white blood cells fill my mouth.

I rolled over onto my back as my mind swayed from mouth pain to leg. I almost disbanded the thought of the attacking creature until I watched the glass axe plummeting downward towards my belly. With tremendous haste I cocked my weapon up at the ready and commanded Sty to take out the glass axe. He did so in a beautiful array of fluttering prisms dancing about with reflective silhouettes of me and the colliding burlap sack wearing being. Glass shattered around my body and cut my flesh as a large piece crushed my left foot breaking every bone to jelly. The numb security of my body kicked in as my spine contained all messages sent to my brain. The enzymes worked hard in my spinal chord jamming up all types of signals.

I turned my body to face the creature head on. Sty's task was finished, it was my turn to inflict pain on this creature. I dug both hands out of defensive mode and turned offensive as I sprayed my emotions out through exerted strength. I neared the monster's left arm as my right fingertips clapped around the handle of the glass axe fragment. With this I batted the creature's hand from grabbing at my face. its hand snapped and cracked like a stepped on bag of cereal. its right arm tried to shield its face from my downward blow but succeeded in nothing. I used the hand to my advantage adding more weight and force to my strike as the back of its hand drove directly into the extended upper jaw and nose of the creature. Again and again I smashed the glass into the head of the creature causing blackish tar to smolder out of every orifice. I watched in an outer body like sitcom episode me splitting the creature's head in two and brain matter accompanied with the bone shell coat the concrete.

It wasn't until the ninth blow to the head of the creature that my spinal chord's work had tired out and the pain signals overwhelmed my brain sending me into a dizzy haze of blur. Through the haze I watched a creature approaching steadily. My body ached uncontrollably. I did nothing. My eyes gave way. Everything was black.

I awoke to the feeling of red hot pliers to my flesh twisting and burrowing into my flesh. The feeling came from the third degree burns on my upper thigh. I watched as the creature that had its head blown off was now occupied by Theodore. Theodore had his head up on top of the dead body and used it to move about taking care of my wounds.

Theodore smiles as friendship hissed from his smile, "These are pretty bad. I did what I can, but you need to find help. I liked how you handled all of that. You scared off the rest after taking out their juggernaut. They were playing with your mind. I could tell from the hook you left me at. But all will be okay. We just need to find you someone who can heal human wounds."

I will not make you a liar God. Punish me, I have sinned, more then once. John taught me this, not to be afraid to address my sins for if I ask for forgiveness it shall be forgotten. Forgotten by God, but not by me. The voiceless faces stain my eyes as the fellowship of regret and sorrow attract towards one another and form a pact. The following of Jesus has lead my footsteps nowhere because I have abandoned all teachings. My God has never abandoned me, but why do I so choose to abandon Him? This is my curse, the world I live in has malfunctioned my mind so that all my humble thoughts now conceal themselves in my mitochondria. I am a traitor. Forgive me. Forgive me. Forgive me.

"Forgive me." I mutter this while I am bound by a coil of pain. This is the moment that a friend, someone whom chooses to pop their head up at the worst moments arrived, the nightmare.

Hmm chuna huuh naa, Hmm chuna huuh naa, hmm chuna huuh naa.

My eyes refused to bear witness to what I knew I heard. The Nightmare of mine was rocking back and forth on a massive metal spring attached to a golden brown playground horse. Rust had colonized on its outer rim as outsiders congealed in the hind section of its aluminum casing. The Nightmare wore lower foam trousers made to look like birds feet as suspenders held them onto his scarred gray body. Over this Nightmares head was a metallic cylinder around the face only revealing the eyes, the first time I've ever seen them. The rest of the cylinder revealed just wet dripping paint from a fake smile on the exterior. His head was tucked up into his chest cavity as he continued to sway the toy back and forth.

Hmm chuna huuh naa, Hmm chuna huuh naa, hmm chuna huuh naa.

The floor below me became nothing but eyeballs twittering and connected in unison as they watched everything all at once. "See my world Blink. We combine greed, hunger, living, and death. I shine a light on all miscommunications this world has with everything else. Do you really believe that THEY really do anything to you? I am your monster, I am your nightmare. It is pathetic how you keep trying to end something that has no real position at all. They are here. I give you that much. But tell me Blink, do they really have all that much control over my actions… or yours? You've gone pretty rouge now haven't you? You have really went on quite a murder spree. Are you still alive? Yes. Is this really hell? Blink? Do you really want to fight me? Why don't we just join forces and hurt others, we can have a joyous adventure into a future of pure torture and mayhem."

The white paint from the Nightmare's mask dripped from the brim of the cylinder's chin. its bead like eyes rummaged the area until they locked onto my eyes since I had now risen from the floor and propped up my upper torso with my left elbow.

My upper lip snarled into a curled correlation of my true feelings, "I am here to stop evil, any form of it. God has…"

The rocking horse ceased immediately as the Nightmare dove his entire body towards the floor of eyes. His hands stabbed into the mulch of vision first as he kept his body risen from impacting the living ground with immense force. He cushioned his landing with a blanket of steady arrival. Once his body touched the eyes completely his movement became erratic as he jerked his head around like a tambourine.

"God? You think God is doing anything? Do you still believe a God exists? I knew you were pathetic. You still believe in hocus pocus and wizards and magic. Did a dragon ever speak of its dealings with God?" The Nightmare's eyes forced beams of light to masquerade as being that of a non intrusive leer.

"He who does not love does not know God. For God is love." The retaliation of mine did not hit with a blow of any kind but enraged his temper.

The acrylic paint diverted its path downward and transferred itself upward as a smile digressed the conversation, "My skin aches with the deception I am faced with. I need your help Blink. You see I could be quite an annoyance. To you... to others as well. You see I have an annoyance also that I need... terminated. But you see I can not get close enough to do any damage."

Pain collapsed into my spinal chord as the river of pain swarmed my brain. "Why would I ever choose to serve you?"

The Nightmare evaporated into a gold precipitation that soared over each eyeball coating it evenly while words echoed throughout the land. "I can heal you." The eyes twitched and spiraled about rapidly in every direction. The air turned hollow reverberating all noises back and forth in a compilation of echolocation.

Blink laid on the blanket of living optical spheres. His breathing fished for a cure for his contaminating spurts of pain. His muscle fluctuations repeated themselves as the inflammation of his wounds proceeded to infect all broken piece of tissue. Paralysis stiffened his left side while aggravation congealed in his cerebellum.

Voices trickled off the surrounding hooks and objects within the room, "Hey, Theodore? Is that you?" A heavy set voice lashed out first towards Blink's new friend. A fine tuned harmonic voice accompanied behind the first boisterous voice. "Hey shut on up there. That is of course Theodore he's just missing some parts."

Theodore leaned using the new body to propel his head towards the approaching noise. "Together Proud!"

The two voices replied with a simultaneous laugh, "Together Proud!"

Stampeding into view for Theodore both Haden and Seal steamed approving emotions over their faces, which were conjoined at the head. Each face laid one on top of the other to make one head.

With sudden impact the corrosive nature of the new creature's smell wafted into Blink's nasal passages. It gnawed at the inner lining of his senses. Through this smell Theodore and Haden and Seal communicated. Theodore secreted a lime trickled stench into the air replying to Haden's stomach acid rotting egg question. Seal laughed with eager haste as peach and molding watermelon spiraled into the air.

A stifled question arose under a steam of burning rubber in Haden's exchange in the conversation of smells. Theodore peeled a smile across his lips as a mint like smell fished for Haden's approval. Seal complied with Theodore's attempt and grimaced as a peppermint like smell accompanied Theodore. Haden shrugged along with Seal.

"Fine," Haden murmured under a salivating tongue. "we will offer this human some aid. You did call us here. We will comply." A massive cylinder shaped tongue extruded Haden's mouth and swiveled its way down to Blinks right arm and lashed out sinking its teeth deep into the muscle evaluating Blink's current condition. Haden's face puckered up as sour emotions exhaled themselves from his facial fluctuations. Seal spoke for his lower half, "This one will die. The wounds are not massive but for a quick fix we will eventually end his life sooner. After the process he will have 3000000 heart beats till his heart devours itself. That is about 3 days for a human being, that is if he doesn't get excited or anxious. I applaud you Theodore, you know how to keep yourself entertained." Haden smirked with delight looming from its eyes. "First lets put him out."

Alternative Medicine.

One day consists of 86,400 seconds. Normally this means nothing to me. A normal human being takes 28,880 breaths a day. What a minuscule number to depend on. On average a body generates 60 to 100 heart beats a minute. That number sounds extremely high, almost like it is an over taking shadow creeping into my soul and stealing it. I am fully healed, but at the cost of this healing I am now going to die. I was always destined to die but now I know the time left for this body. I can feel within my arms a power that will dwindle as I blink.

It was eight hours ago since Theodore broke this new dying news to my ears. Thanks, friend. Sarcasm files down that statement of mine and tries to make it harmful but is not. I am thankful for the chance to finish my task. I will not reconcile to the thought of the human race melting under the pressure of reform, annihilation.

I never weaned my emotions with a happy catalyst. I forced it to mature, grow up before it was ready. Now the body that is dwindling curses my intentions and begs me to show some kind of compassion by granting it these last days to die in peace. The failing prophet in my heart said it was the end of time like bringing about judgment day was a plan of mine. It tells me to watch the pages turn as each page marks a passage of time tearing life from my soul.

I count each pulse of my heart. Each one twists the dial closer to death. I feel childlike as I pray the summer would not end and forebode the day school starts. I have a payment due to God and this will be collected soon but not until after I am finished. I am the shadow of death's cast out upon those who will soon meet him head on.

The smirk plastered to my cheeks reveal a story. The story is a complicated rift of why I am currently wearing a green and black plaid jump suit and have a metallic spider like contraption the size of my hand halfway buried into my right shoulder blade. The spider has a blue and red liquid that is separated but when some oddity tells it to, the liquids will merge into another tube and become injected into the spider's drone. Then festively the drone will erupt into pieces after reaching the heart.

Here is the story.

After my awakening into this realm of being a time watcher I proceeded to drain Theodore of all his knowledge on any subject resulting in destroying the nightmare. His response was mediocre and annoying because it did not help my pursuit one bit. So I limped my way to the closest daycare. You see there is a being that protects the children in the city his name is Calm. This was a way of weeding out what individuals I needed to complete my task. I decided to hold the children hostage, tied them up and hid them in a corner. Then that is when it got a tiny bit interesting. The point Calm decided to enter the commotion is when the police did not seem to get a response from me. I had barricaded up all windows with arts and craft tables along with covering each door with construction paper and locking them. This was my crime scene, I owned the situation. I actually believe that Calm entered this hostage situation because I became cocky at one moment and decided to pop a round of Sty's into a police vehicle causing it to implode around the gas tank and tear open the trunk. If shots are fired towards a police official they tend to cry and call in the big dogs, in this instance they chose to call in one man, Calm. That was exactly what I wanted.

Calm is a man who has a shotgun strapped to the outside of his right arm and a trigger pull system connected to his right hand finger tips. He wore a leather wanderer's hat which resembled a more modernized version of a 1875 wild west outlaw's hat. Upon his chest he wore a black short sleeved "T" shirt and a vest over it with pockets filled with ammunition for his weapon. His left hand bore a stainless steel wrist guard that trailed off to each finger of his and covered each tip making a claw on each finger.

When Calm comes into a situation you can guarantee that he is going to be anything but calm. He is a walking icon of irony. With his gutsy attitude he strolled right through the wall I ripped open to frighten the police by destroying a vehicle. So he enters grinning as he notices the children huddled in the corner area where all their lunches and backpacks get stored and sorted.

To allow full understanding of how everything went down I will change my blunt rendition of the situation.

Writhing in a clear headed incorruptible stance Calm positioned himself at a quarter turn to my infamous seeming projection. I blundered over thoughts of how to address this man and how to convert what image he's been bombarded with and revamp it to help seeking human being. I clawed at the bottom of the bucket trying to dig out the last remaining ideas. Nothing would come out of my mouth, nothing would reveal my true nature to this iconic symbol of good and justice.

The pistons of tension fired off within the daycare molding all the minds of the children's into a faithless fearsome pile of mush susceptible of anything. The washable paint and crayon drawings pasted all over the room created an ominous landscape of zeal but the interlaced glares of mine and Calm's remained that of pure malcontent and hostility.

Calm's demeanor lashed out with a verbal attack, "Children, what purpose does this serve?"

I was poisoned by the image of me he has caste over my body and I sprinted along with it under my arm pit, "I've watched them suffer before. There is nothing new here."

Calm retaliated with a vulgarity laced within his teeth, "Nothing new, holding innocence at gunpoint is nothing new?"

This last statement of his bounded within my brain causing irregularities in my thinking process. Evil, evil is a manifestation of society along with taboos. No, what if the truest form of evil is something you are born with, good is the manifestation of society. Good is something people strive for, but evil is something easily performed without any hardship or barricade. In a sense there is nothing but evil in the children but their parents could have ingrained good into their minds with an intellectual chisel, or by a hand held one, I've seen it both ways.

I maintained my composure as the words flowed poetically from my lips, "Evil begot these children, they were born in Hell, and ended up being raised in Hell. How is my actions any different then the actions these monsters will ultimately perform?"

With the nudge of his head I realized Calm became infuriated by my comment and question. His adrenaline blazed into his capillaries and enflamed the muscles. "There is no hidden meaning behind this, just a man playing God with children."

Reality split my melodramatic façade in two as I rekindled my natural way of thinking, but the damage has been done. Calm is a man of little words, I missed my chance. The fire fight began.

I tasted a grainy dryness of rust brush against my tongue as a hue of light blue set the tone of our beginning moments together. In the first few moments before a round exits any chamber there is always a connection, a bond between each opposing force. I knew more about himself then he wanted to expose, the same goes for him, if he was perceptive.

The thought of using children to my advantage for cover ravaged my mind. I could blossom into something hellacious and ride this spiritless act to the grave by coating each wall with the blood of fearful youth. I came for information not devastation. I could remove their faces and hollow out their cranium and place a mirror in place so that each child will harbor my image and my face. Can their be too much honor in standing up for an act, it seems that this fake persona is wanting to take hold of my body indefinitely and corrupt what sensibility and morals I have.

I will not fire a round, but I can not let him hit me or get me too excited. Calm's finger pulled upon the elaborate trigger system, at this moment I realized the extent of my doing. I must conquer a tank without becoming a victim and find a way out of the predicament I've created.

On impulse I threw my body over to my right hand side trying to secure myself behind a long narrow kitchen area where the food preparation is conducted. With my bound the wall behind me splintered out loosing mass as children screamed and wept with all their lung's capacity of might. I stretched my palms out ahead of me to catch myself on the black and white checkered tiles but in accidental positioning I flicked the trigger of Sty's upon landing. The oven beside my right earlobe imploded through the wall and out into the street. The police officials upon hearing the commotion inside readied their weapons and aimed them at the daycare.

Assault after assault exploded from the shotgun and lopped off chunks of the open kitchen counter top known as an island. Entrapping my presence Calm ripped holes in both sides of the island narrowing my escape. I peeked my head around the corner of my island and watched Calm steadily walking closer. I devised an escape as I circled my weapon out ahead of me and towards the kitchen's far end wall and I dismantled it in one of Sty's well placed hiccups.

The hole in the far wall smoldered with floating particles of debris as it revealed a compressor. The compressor smiled from under loose strands of plaster and dry wall. I reached over across from me and plugged in an extension chord into an outlet. The roar of the compressor startled the children whom were tied up.

I raised abruptly pointing my friend out ahead of me towards Calm offering him a revelation of possibilities. I chose not to fire, perfect opportunity to end his life. I held in my left hand a tube connected to a valve which latched itself onto the end of the compressor. The other end of this rubber tube, to Calm's dismay, was hidden away in one of the hostage's chest cavity.

The stalemate compelled sweat to swarm Calm's upper lip as I twitched my lips back and forth without precipitation, "You see I could harm two people right now, a child, and you. But I offer a solution. You hear me out. How does that sound?"

Anger caused pressure to build within Calm's head as his face swelled with a reddening glaze, "Proceed."

A stern rash of my act fading from the scene stiffened my presence and my words, "I need directions. I have a limited amount of time and need a new heart. I am not sure what alien material is inside of me but I don't trust Them touching it. I need someone with special expertise. Help me."

An unpleasant to myself smile passed Calm's cheeks, "You were given the synthetic heart. You're nothing more then a lost cause. Let me guess, you're staging this entire hostage situation. Nice. But you're not going to be permitted to leave these walls."

This is when I felt deep inside a monster take hold and rip my morals into shreds, "I am sorry you feel that way." My heartbeat escaladed into a tantrum of rage.

My thumb twisted the compressor on as a child screamed in agony from my left peripheral. Calm's face streaked into a worry shell as I asked Sty politely to cough in the direction of Calm. Calm's reflexes were stifled but still grasped enough time to evade the first strike of Sty's as the entire wall behind Calm paraded into the next adjacent room.

Calm's evasion warped his presence into the enclosed staircase to the living rooms of the daycare's owner. I banished two cannon blasts into the stair's surrounding wall but both missed Calm entirely, by how close I am not sure, but from his reaction it must have been less then inches. Plaster and drywall encased his body while he recovered in his step engrossed security.

When Calm finally decided to join my company once more he found me coaching the children how to line up in a single file line. The child screaming from the compressor filling his lungs with air did not stop from vomiting as it lashed out from the inside emotion's rage. I placed my left hand in the air grabbing on to the roller coaster of loathing soon to reap the image of horror soon to pass. I squeezed on Sty's stress struck trigger which impaled the first child in the cranium causing it to burst like a firework of skull and brain matter, the second child stood wrongfully taller then the first so her neck untangled itself into a confetti of flesh. The third and the fourth child copied one another thoroughly by cracking directly down the middle and splashing to each side with escaping entrails. The last child chose to be intact and completely different as she rocketed backwards into the air causing a collision with body mass and wall but her miniature structure could not hold that much stress and shattered under the pressure.

From this point on Calm collapsed into a woeful ocean of regret. I could not understand why I did such a horrific action. I dropped Sty, injuring my friend. A monster, that is what I became. You must have the monster inside of you to live in these times, but I became a monster to stand up for what? I murdered children, for no reason.

The police handcuffed me after forcefully subduing me and beating my body full of bruises. This pain did not matter. The pain I felt inside for what I've become, betraying my God. That pain outweighed everything mankind could inflict.

Come, ye children, hearken unto me: I will teach you the fear of the LORD. Psalm 34:11

Story that lead me here ends.

My sins are great numbering far beyond those needed to access the furthest realm of Hell. I've ended the lives of the innocent, I have loosened the bolts on all knowledge and teachings of the Lord. What purpose do I deserve to continue on and help mankind, am I helping anyone?

So this is my prison. I am in a box, walls painted black, and my clothes checkered in black and green. I also now live with a spider like beast in my back for security purposes till my trial. Do I wait here and die? Do I fight? Do I escape? Do I attempt to find another heart, or do

I find another alternative medicine to my plight? Right now I prepare. I feel the thorns coming on.

Nightmares approach.

Through an aluminum loud speaker up at the far end of my sightless room I heard an all familiar voice. "How are we today, young man? Don't answer that. I already know. So let me figure something out about you. You pretend to disregard everything I ask of you, and you then run off and try to do what? Find a person whom doesn't know shit. Why don't you just do what I asked of you? Let me tell you things will be a lot more simpler. Don't turn away from the speaker or shake your head in anger. I ask this as a friend. I am one whom enjoys your company, I don't want to harm you. If you keep up this unresponsive nature of yours I just might have to give you some incentive."

From the abyss raised a clear plastic container. Locked up hidden behind the container was Sty and Amy both completely unharmed and intact. "Let me make this simple. You can leave whenever you want. Just for this incontinence you owe me seven pounds of flesh, for your weapons and the key to leave. Be patient and see how hunger makes this offer become quite ... tasty."

The loud speaker ceased any noise. I felt my willpower raise up for the occasion and rebel against the nightmare's words. I will not do this. I will not remove seven pounds of my flesh for this creature. The floor leers into my skin with cold extracts. The only smell I can comprehend is my own sweat from the greasy nature of my emotions.

This is deception. Why would I have a security measure on my back? What is it this creature wants from me? It refuses to stop and let me die in peace. Or is it trying to raise my pulse, kill me in another way. It wants to watch me mutilate my body as nothing happens afterwards and my escape never happens. I will die here. I will die if I loose my mind. How will I escape? How does this place work? I must leave soon. How?

I must use my senses. I must rekindle my knowledge about the surroundings. Think, just think about what you're in. I have at my finger tips the loud speaker and... suddenly with a shock wave a high pitched shrill came over the loud speaker. My body lost all mobility as I became a pile of chewed bubble gum on the cell's floor. A noise sizzled through the sealed entry way, "Lunch Time."

Lunch time, it is nothing more then a mockery of our intelligence as human beings. Like runts in the cattle we are escorted from our holding tank so we can secrete the milk of hunger and sorrow into a window pane of pain. This window pane is a layered compilation of suicidal emotions, guilt, poisonous threats, and dried red blood cell accruements. It is a room, a room with just windows to darkness and one by one we are required to let it all out. The puss within my pimpled existence has come to a head and now I am ready to pop.

My turn inside the chamber. There is nothing but my mirrored image. Me, myself, my image, and my reflection. Four windows reveal the deepest darkest secrets of my soul. I challenge them all by doing nothing. The pulse in my blood never accumulates or diminishes. I am an army of frozen stones without a warm bead to feast on. All that has been happening to me has only taken away and taken away. There has to be something to put in this void some call a soul or else it becomes nothing more then a dead star that soon collapses into a black hole.

"We must collect something from this one."

The foreign voice of a being unseen echoes throughout the room.

Submerged in the darkness a wild cascade of laughter erupted and rolled down the floor to my feet.

I spun around with a steady turn to offer my captives. I dangled my hands and body in gird. My laxity was put to the test as soon as I witnessed seven children standing against the far mirrored wall all with bags over their heads and shredded clothing. From under each bag was a medley of blood and laughter as each one of the children's body quaked with humor driven actions. My glare propelled forward sinking into each paper mask notifying the children of my mental stability.

"Hello, Blink." Child one nodded his head in coupling with the others whom also joined in.

"I am a futuristic parasite here for your liking." Child two sounded off in unison.

"The sickening of our children is for you to over look." Child three pressed her two palms together in a prayer pose.

"Come father try to get inside." Child four screamed his words with a flurry of clawing the overhanging air.

"Come mother peel us as we hide." Child five crossed her arms with a pout and a sliver of sadness.

"We've made a monolith of our emotions." Child six raised her arms high above her head to demonstrate her words.

"So we set fire to our faces and watch it burn." Child seven breathed a demonic essence through his bag. "We are seven. We will make your nightmares… real."

A strained breath of amusement telecasted itself into these children's senses. In comparison I feel like a grain of diastases which is capable of turning starch into dextrose, I am capable of turning emotions into fuel for my soul to feast upon. I devour emotions and gain nutrition, the dietetic me.

The fourth child screamed as blood poured profusely from under the bag. He fell backwards onto his rump clinging to the mirrored window behind him. The bag rose upward as beneath it bulged a set of massive antlers ripping the bag like tissue paper. The bag flaked away and revealed a massive head of a caribou attached to a child's neck. The caribou whelped as its flesh peeled upward off its cheeks revealing bone and muscle. The caribou face gagged shaking about gazing up at me begging for a miniature amount of emotion and concern. Anger conveyed itself through the creature's eyes.

With a convulsion of anger the child ripped its horns out screaming through its caribou face as blood coated the child's shoulders like two spouts draining human waste. The blood splashed about not coating or coming in contact with the other children whom remained unmoved. The caribou face tilted with happiness as it proceeded to gaze into my eyes. All of a sudden the lights began to blink. The caribou remained unflinching as darkness pulsed with the beat of my heart. Testing the darkness and my pulse the caribou leaned to the far left, the child's body seemed eager to pounce on me but remained in control.

The male child hands reached forward digging into the muzzle of the caribou face. Fragments of the nostril tore off and feathered away into the darkening abyss. The nails of the child's made sure to scrape the flesh clean off the bone so that the end of the caribou face was nothing more then tendons and bone. The face roared with laughter leaning forward with a chuckle.

With one heartbeat of darkness there was a sudden scene change and now I laid on a bed with mirrors all around me reflecting the light of the moon above. The light bounced around the room coating the overhanging child with the caribou face whose standing on a stool of folded up flesh. The boy's hands were placed up on either side of the caribou face as his fingers were wiggling about and his mouth jetted open and shut. With a final furry of force the caribou's eyes shriveled up and sunk back into the head. The moonlight painted a white faint coating of ominous hatred on the hair coating beneath the eye sockets.

I lifted my upper torso and smiled wide at the caribou face. I used my right hand and placed my fingers up under the lower mandible and clung to the loose flap of skin pulling the face closer to mine. "The difference between you and me are you pretend to be a monster, I am one."

The child screamed with the caribou face as he tried to pull away. I refused to let him go as I clutched the head as hard as I could pulling it closer to me. its tiny arms poked and prodded at my shoulders and chest trying to gain some kind of upper hand but I allowed no counter attack. I squeezed the head trying to crumple the bone into the brain mass and destroy the conscious being beneath, but I propelled the creature ahead of be so the back of its head collided with the mirror.

The room reverted itself back into the previous state and the caribou child sunk low into a growling upset fit. I remained standing in a readied poise. The child rose from the floor and returned to its fourth in line position.

My body slumped over to the left taking in all the loathing through osmosis. "Pathetic."

Suddenly with the entertainment of my answer the seven children laughed as hard as they could. Each head wobbled about energetically including the caribou, but their bodies remained unflinching.

Child one slid his right palm against his chest as if petting an animal, "I am doing nothing but amusing myself."

Child two stretched his arms up over his head in a yawn, "Because we get awfully tired of the same old creatures day in and day out."

The third child pulled a heart from her pocket and placed it up underneath her paper bag and removed it demonstrating her hunger by showing a half severed heart. "I'm hungry aren't you?"

With her words ending a stained pair of upper and lower jaws erupted from beneath the bag along with a bag of flesh attached to her neck. The bag remained tearless as the teeth rocked back and forth getting situated. Her jaws repelled one another opening up to allow an elongated tongue to sliver out ahead of her face. The tongue glided across each tooth leaving a morose ooze behind.

Ahead of her a body congealed itself as it hung by its legs from the ceiling. Her tongue stretched itself out to touch the face of the body. The body had flesh sagging from its bones and was a purple tint because of rigamortis. During rigamortis the body is unable to disband the conjunction between the myosin and actin creating a perpetual state of muscular contraction, that is until the breakdown of muscle tissue by the digestive enzymes in decomposition. The state of the body caused it to remain completely unmovable and resembling the upright position.

The girl licked the delicate fibers of flesh of the body as the teeth slowly proceeded to either side of the face. The tongue touched the nostrils with sensual intentions as both jaws clapped together removing the flesh and bone from the head and allowing the enzymes from within to spill upon her bag and chest as she rubbed her hands in it.

My mouth opened as I felt my tongue help birth words, "I find peace in pain and suffering. No matter what images you show me, I will not feel. I don't know my family, I don't know my past. Nothing of that sort can be shown to me and rekindle a reaction. I am a vault of emptiness. I am here to consume your attempts. You should release me."

Child one turned to his left and so did the second child. The third child fell to her knees while the fifth and the sixth did the same. The caribou raised his hands to the ceiling in a praying stance as the seventh child stepped ahead out of line.

The seventh child placed one foot ahead of the other as he headed up to be directly ahead of Blink, "Today I admit to someone a fault. This was not my current intention. I do not mean to harm another human being. I wish with all my being to destroy its psyche. I want to take down the construct of their mainframe and rewire it entirely. But this I can not do to you. So what can I do to you? You see I pretend to be a child. Several children to be exact, but you… what is it about you that makes you so inhuman? Not human. You have performed an aberration, you have deviated from the moral course of what is right and wrong. Let me offer you a moral imperative. Not all nightmares you encounter are real, but some are… and that makes things a wee bit more terrifying in your eyes. To know that your worst nightmares are actually out running about doesn't seem that safe does it, specimen 92? We don't find many of you… were abit more guarded then average. its hard to come here."

My head ached with a rove of minuscule thoughts until one nestled itself in the web of rationalization, "Do you… child seven stay in hiding because you fear someone," I placed my hand up feeling a panic entangle my fingertips. "You are not human nor one of them. You're a nightmare like the one who hired me."

I stepped forward with all my might and picked up the boy to my eye level muttering, "When thou goest forth to war against thine enemies, and the Lord thy God hath delivered them into thine hands, and thou hast taken them captive… You young nightmare will feel death today."

A haze of laughter and an orange smog fluttered throughout the room. "You know nothing… I am destruction itself."

Immediately following his last words his skin slumped down to the floor below offering a blanket of fake sewn flesh. Dripping with coagulated yellow grease the seventh child revealed its true body. It was a concoction of all the children together, number one and five made up the legs of the beast. The legs were clothed like children each still wearing the paper mask which connected to the other five children making up the rest of the body. The face was the caribou all gnarled and vicious. The lower jaws was child three.

With a sudden explosion of intestines from its stomach area they stretched across the entire room lashing out ingraining itself into each wall. His body moaned with his flesh reeking with impending malicious intent. The two massive facial tissue hands of his steamed close to one another then embraced to laud, praising the unseen act about to arise. I bore witness to the ceiling transforming itself into a porous flesh like texture. Along the middle of the ceiling tissue there was a hole two foot in diameter.

I leered into the hole with bewilderment when to my surprise an armless blood covered being jetted out chomping its only incisors at my face. All the creature was that came from the ceiling was a body and a massive head and two large sets of incisors nipping at my cranium. I hunched down evading the attack when up from the floor came a maroon tentacle, which found its way directly to my neck and encircled my neck cutting off air and blood circulation. I erected my body placing immense strain on my neck as my cheeks blood vessels erupted from the strain. The cones in my eyes relinquished their command over my sight and allowed darkness to cascade over my vision. I heard the creature from the ceiling propel itself downward towards my head again but this time I leaned backwards allowing it to sink the incisors into the tentacle. The plan devised in moments worked perfectly without flaws, my body agreed to cooperate with me once more and jumpstarted my vision and mobility to maximum adrenaline absorbed power.

I quickly gazed at the lower extremities of the monstrosity and feasted upon the image of the antlers which were torn from the caribou's head. With a swift dive of determination I leapt my way through an onslaught of tentacles and warped my right hand around the base of a large antler. My new weapon caused my foe to quake with anger while sharply polishing out screams of diamond shattering intensity. The creature tore free from the walls and grinned my direction with the skinless muzzle it possessed. I raised it up over my head to strike the caribou's face straight on but instead I found my chest floating as my body traveled horizontally downward. A tentacle had scooped my feet from under my body causing my upper torso to collapse against the ground.

The tentacle pinched my legs together and raced me backwards towards the far wall furthest from the antler and the seventh child. I wailed my fingernails against the floor trying to gain the upper hand and offer some kind of resistance. All of a sudden I was hoisted into the air upside down, the blood drained to my head causing spots to envelope my eyesight and stain my retina. I watched as the seventh child raced head first bucking wildly towards my face in a ramming position. I dropped my hands out ahead of me to brace for impact and maybe catch the creature's face. Along my fingertips I flinched at the carnivorous skin pricking hair upon its face, but I impaled my thumbs into its eyeless eye sockets ceasing its furry.

It reached up scratching and clawing at my neck tearing the first few layers of my flesh from my collar. I composed an attack using my abs as I bent at the waist carrying the creature's body by his head. I drove it straight towards the massive hole in the ceiling which excited the hovel's inhabitant. Out from the hole immerged the blissful aforethought which took a bite out of the right brain vicinity. The pain from the daft creature in the cavern allowed the monster controlled tentacle a loose grip so me squirming my body from its grasp was nothing more then a counter turn of my vessel.

I extended my arms and wielded the antler as a blade. This was my final strike to the monstrosity. I impaled the throat with a mild sized end of the antler, this opened a four inch gateway to drain out what life source there was inside the creature.

Child seven pried one of the tendons back allowing the caribou face to smile once more as he spat out a few more syllables before death plagued his soul, "You have no idea what you… have done. He is going to … be… s…s… stronger."

This is my carnal tomb, seek the lusts of life. I have palatable passion for my intentions but lack the presence of cyanide within my veins. I need to die one way or another. God, He with all His majesty keeps me alive. I dance my grievances into a present which covertly lies beneath a tree for Him to unwrap. I feel remorse but also I feel acceptance by Him. I have requested for His forgiveness and feel less of a man. Not because I am filled with less pride and or mass but because I am filled with less doubt, less woe, and less sorrow. I've taken a fire to my emotions in order to scab the wound and hide it from sight, but the presence of the pain still remains hidden beneath a thin blanket of cover. I am sorry God. You have tried to fill me with morals and I have spilled them time and time again. Never will I drink this cup of serenity. I congeal inside a fiery bottle of gasoline. Maybe this is my path. I must be this way so that I can pull off such a feat. I follow your bidding. I will continue my mission, my heart's mission. Maybe this is how you speak to us, not from listening with our minds but through our hearts. My heart tells me there is a lot more left to finish off.

This is all I have needed all along. My heart maybe dying but there is something else growing stronger inside. A light in an eternal darkness can still reveal hope. I have formed a new understanding, a new bond. I have found an alternative means of medicine.

GENOCIDE.

Prothesis is a being forever laying upon its back which has the ability to transmit data from one being to the next as they die, the data being a soul. The brother to Prothesis is Ekphora which prepares the soul to go onward into the entrapment they have conjured. The two brothers built a tomb engraved with the Phoenician script to collect and imprison excavated souls from their flesh coated vessel.

I have met these two people in my previous attempts of a life. To be exact I have no proof or recollection of these two but my mind wrestles with déjà vu. I pound the resourcefulness of my mind into a six foot deep grave and top it off with a headstone that reads "Dormant and deceased". I find my right index finger twitching in repetition but can not find the second piece in its puzzle, Sty.

In the human body the brain is made up of four cross sections; anterior, superior—dorsal, inferior—ventral, and posterior. Anger begins to build inside the anterior section in the ventral area of the prefrontal cortex but judging on how strong this emotion is it might actually break through the crucial restrains for impulsive outbursts located in this region. This describes my current status while slumped over checking the vital signs of this creature I've just condemned.

After this room in the prison I am suppose to be hauled off to a separate facility entirely where Prothesis and Ekphora would passionately remove any spirit left inside my carcass. I found this vital piece of information by continuing the route. I exited the room using the antler for one last task and continued on the path of destruction laid out for us inmates.

There was a hallway entangled with rows of eyeballs all impaled on the spikes of razor wire. The air inside the hallway hammered fear into the occupant's head with the aroma of unwanted pain and suffering. The ceiling was paved in tar and sapphire pebbles. At the end of the hallway was a building branched off from all the rest of the prison. This is where the brothers Prothesis and Ekphora dwell. Unknowingly my actions within the previous room have tripped a silent alarm allowing all the inhabitants in the prison to know my actions and location, and also unknown to myself Sty awaited me inside this room.

The entry way into the structure was through a polyester like flap of skin. Directly on the opposing side of the flap there was Ekphora, he held a weapon and a satchel of ammo, my best friend Sty. Behind Ekphora laid Prothesis whom smiled wide with sand infested gums.

Ekphora placed my friend into my arms and laughed, "Take it," Ekphora's eyes changed color instantly to a dull white. The beasts hand raised upward pointing back behind me towards the other rooms. "Enter ... tain... ment."

This is the reason the nightmare of mine wasn't able to enter the prison. The prison is heavily guarded with creatures ready to die instantly for their headmasters cause. Sty buzzed with warmth causing adrenaline to rocket through my arteries sending my pulse into an all out frenzy. The combination of friendship and destruction was lavished by my right arm and tasted by my spirit.

Hearing the stampede of feet heading my way I turned to the wall beside me and removed it from existence with one twitch of my right index finger. Light entombed my body as the sun welcomed my presence. I blinked a slow progressive eye latching so that salted lubricant could cover my eyes and prepare them for action. I placed one foot in front of the other and shattered the bind darkness had on my body.

Blink stepped with all his force onto the still shimmering dew coated grass. The grass coated a junkyard of demolished airplanes, ripped apart vehicles, and a mall made out of corpses. The Boeing 777 in the center had a half way carved out fuselage and was strung up from each wing tip to a wall of bodies. The junk yard spanned ten acres across and was bordered with thirty foot tall walls of bodies and brick. On each corner of the boundaries stood an armed guard with mirrored face masks and body armor.

Blink's arms raised over head as he absorbed the heat and love from the sun, "Fight the good fight of the faith. Take hold of the eternal life to which you were called."

Over a loud speaker the sound of screeches and screams frosted the yard. Blink's body tensed up feeling his body growing stronger with each beat of his heart, his index finger tickled the brow of Sty's. Deep inside Blink knew this stand could be his last, this worry passed itself on to Sty through osmosis. Sty counteracted Blink's worries by evening out temperatures between the two bodies. They will work as one.

No sound could be heard by Blink as splashes of sparks painted an aura around his body. The condemned brick structure on top of the half bed of a rusted over truck peeled away with every bullet collision. The brick splintered off into tiny missile like fragments which stung Blink's back causing him to snap out of his daze.

Once in full cooperation with his conscious self Blink darted towards a Concorde jet wing for protection. The softball sized eruptions of dirt and grass from each penetrating shot covered Blink's feet as he raced to cover. Blink found cover behind the wing as mallet like blows bombarded the opposing side of the wing which was propped up by the nose of a hollowed out Airbus A380 and cockpit.

Above all the HK416 assault rifle fire was a wild hissing roar in the rear direction of Blink. Approaching Blink with an onslaught of malice a seven foot tall halfway cloaked beast wielding a three foot wide hammer and blessed with a face that has been maimed and charred. Blink saw the charge from the creature and also noticed the pile of vehicles beside him. A cannon blast echoed through out the yard as the bottom vehicle tore out from under the other two causing a collapse of metal to strike down the charging beast. The beast was struck in the left knee by a chrome bumper which set the creature up for the twisting vehicle on its hood to slide forward crushing the creature's face into the side of the Airbus A380's cockpit.

A rumbling of thunder rolled from the same direction of Blink's entrance onto the junk yard plain. Blink swooped up his friend and directed it towards the transitioning hole. The thunder continued to tremble the ground as the HK416's ceased firing.

The jubilation of five crazed prisoners out ahead of a hundred more, all held weapons crafted from objects within their cells. A steaming cough from Sty sent the first five prisoners into an explosion of meaningless antics of hatred. The entire civilian status of prisoners tried fitting through a five foot wide hole, they bottlenecked. This gave Blink a moment to think as he gazed upon the left wing of the Boeing 777 which was attached by a threaded metallic fiber and strung up to a pile of bodies overhanging the bottlenecking hole of prisoners. Two enormous echoes rocked the walls of the yard and imploded the far wall of bodies of interlaced metallic fibers, which were ingrained into the bodies which caused them to become disemboweled from the implosion.

This caused the Boeing 777's wing to tilt downward almost scraping the grass below. Blink turned and capped off two more rounds of Sty's into the far back end of the Boeing causing it to sway back and forth. The rocking caused the Boeing's wing to swing through the hole bashing limbs and bodies together causing death to some inmates.

The back end of the Boeing 777 branded its paint coating with Blink's Concorde wing cover and caused it to teeter to the left and off the Airbus A380's nose. This accident exposed Blink to the HK416's held by the armed patrol men on the walls. Blink's surroundings exploded with gunfire causing the ground to become mulched as he rolled his way under the left tilted teetering wing of the Boeing. The wing absorbed a few minor implanted gunshots. Blink raised up too quick after his dive and clocked his left shoulder on the open panel for raising and lowering the landing gear. This impact hurled Blink to the grassy plain below allowing him to become a clear target for the patrol men.

This momentary laps of movement and attack from Blink allowed the prisoners to coat the yard with their presence. A rush of silence spiraled through the yard tearing all fears of Blink's away and wrapping them up with terror.

Across the furthest loud speaker a voice spewed forth in a commanding furry, "The one who kills that prisoner will be pardoned from this prison."

Blink dug Sty's nose into the dirt and propped himself up off the floor as quick as possible to avoid the Boeing. He stumbled forward as a gunshot clapped the end of Sty causing Blink to loose his stance and collapse forward to the passenger side of a gutted out BMW. He surveyed his friend to make sure all is well. Sty had been cracked at the barrel but over all still useful and still able to fight. Blink's teeth grinded together causing a series of forced increments of adrenaline to shower his limbs.

The mob of prisoners suddenly realized the position of Blink and started rushing the region. Blink felt the tower of three vehicles to his back shake violently and the BMW to his left ring out with chalice coated palms slapping against its frame.

Blink raised his gun up and relinquished the last round in the clip towards the upper vehicle in the pile which the force caused it to barrel roll over itself and smash the climbing inmates, the impact tore limbs and collapsed skulls. Blink's left hand quickly aimed to reload Sty as the sight of thirty inmates circling the BMW clashed with his reloading attempts. The first creature to get within five feet of Blink since the beginning of the attack was holding up a very large plastic coated steel bed frame rod. Blink got the new cartridge in the chamber. A smile cascaded through his cheeks as he used Sty to rip the head right off the first closest inmate.

The Boeing 777 rocked its way back towards Blink as he shot the right wing's attachment and end of the wing clear off causing the nose and front end of the fuselage to jet downward at Blink's position. Blink quickly leapt his body into the back seat of the gutted BMW as the plane crushed eight inmates with the fuselage and pinched the structure of the BMW inward.

A barrage of gunfire pounded the rear door frame Blink hid beside. Sparks lighting up the shadowed interior. A silhouette of light and dust created a halo above Blink's head. Anger swept past his aching body as he warped the side of the plane into fragments of its former self using three screams of Sty's. Blink pushed his lower body through the mangled BMW mess and into the Boeing's fuselage.

Inside the fuselage Blink could see rows of seats still completely intact. The inside was morbid and morose but still resembled the vessel it once was. Inside this mechanical beast Blink couldn't help but notice the calm of it all. The tranquil peace of being in an armored monster.

All around the vessel Blink heard sixty hands and weapons beating savagely on the exterior of the Boeing. Blink's eyes met with his friend Sty, his fingers nuzzled at Sty's cheek. "Rise up; this matter is in your hands. We will support you, so take courage and do it."

Blink's right hand supported Sty so that he could reload his friend just to make sure he has enough when things get messy. Blink turned to his right gazing out onto the Boeing's left wing. A shockwave shattered the planes left side wide open as a passage way was now created to its left wing which was tilted up towards the top of the bordering wall. A yell exited Blink as he struck a chord inside his soles and jettisoned his body out into the open. Sunlight bathed him in welcoming arms trying to tell him that everything will be alright. His resting place will be eternally prepared in a comfy setting, but Blink refused to accompany death.

Blink's body scaled the wing as fate wielding rounds hiss by his body trying to describe the death that can be dealt. Blink's front right foot palm touched the end of the wing which was level with the wall's peek. He leapt from it as time seemed to stand still trying to catch its breath as the impossible continued to happen.

Instantly at the clap of two soles against the wall of corpses Blink began to control the scene with an iron fist. He swooped his accompanying weapon towards the closest patrolman as he cracked the sound barrier ahead of the armored individual causing limbs to escape in every direction from fear of what happened to the main central control node. A rogue round impaled Blink's left forearm and he bowed over towards his knees giving way to his legs so that his pelvis could absorb the impact of the fall.

Sty had a mind of its own as he lashed out twice tearing two gunmen from this world before they could hear the bone shattering scream of his. One more attacker with a projectile stood by reloading his only means of joining the conflict. Blink leaned his body over and arm dangling from the side of the wall so that he could aim the friend of his at a line of inmates scaling the Boeing's left wing. A sneeze exited Sty so that the inmates' limbs and bodies dismantled themselves from their owners before being asked to.

Blink then clipped off the end of the wing with two more pulls of Sty's trigger. Several prisoners plummeted to their death while Blink nonchalantly rose from his prone position. With out warning the floor below Blink opened up and he tumbled through the air onto a blood scathed table twenty feet below. He landed knees first and his upper torso second then afterwards his hands and Sty. Pain surged the doors of Blink's body requesting his mind to shut down. Blink's willpower banished all attempts to tear away his coherency. His head cocked itself back and forth surveying the world, it was Prothesis and Ekphora's lair, but besides Ekphora was a head held in his hand, Theodore.

Ekphora reached out cuffing his hand over Blink's mouth and smiling, "We will help you escape, you entertained quite well and shall be rewarded. If you would have passed the wall your body would have exploded from the spider."

Theodore attached his eyes directly into Blink's retina's the friendship between the two revealed itself. Blink's body calmed down a percentage of his pulse.

In this life we can not count on anyone. This was my previous mindset, I have all but changed my mind. I now know there is friendship in this world for me. Even if my friendship has been with an enemy. I have also learned of love. Love that is eternal and always there for me to grasp. He has kept me alive this long, because of my friendship and my belief. Thank you. Thank you for keeping me in your heart and thank you for coming back to help me out. I have never experienced such love. I may be laying in a cesspool of filth but I wouldn't rather be anywhere else. I now have a new weakness but a strength at the same time. I have burnt the old Blink in a fire of caring and love. It is time to bring this world back from the hell it has been cast into.

Fruit Of The Condemned

 I am the inflamed blemish on a skinless corps. I am a weapon of monetary caliber ready to be traded as currency for the Blink lacking diet of an obese plague. I brand my name on each prod of a probing stick used by three children of cursed creature status as I lay a beached jellyfish relinquished of all control.
 The inflorescence of life congealed on my face has formed a bangle of pain around the ankle of my spirit. I am loosing the ancient molding around the decay of my mask. The chipped fragments recede my looming facial landscape. Out from under the filth of a post modern civilization rises a being that has been transformed through myth and legend, something good. Words that fill the world with hope and caring are the sins of yesterday. The passage of the prevailing few morals has been layered with deceit and damnation.
 Inside this box my soul has been screaming away, the darkness light showering my body with decay. My thoughts of positive stature have lashed out with anger trapping them in a negative stain. The darkness realm is sagacious with an eye for all emotions and attempts of escape. The strength, a being I've placed in the background, has given me the chance of reform. A chance to reconcile my difference's and strike the evil down with retribution.

I am accompanied by my friend Theodore as my body lies in a fallen refrigerator hollowed out and kept for storage. Him and I are crammed in a solitude of shadow and forgotten woe. My muscles tense but remain calm around a friendly aura. I compare sets of statements to address him but nothing seems satisfactory so I continue to lay without uttering a syllable.

Sirens yelp as boisterous yelling prances about the prison. They are looking for me. I scratched at the notion of escaping the two creatures and flaring up the inflammation known as death upon the structure. The darkness tends to absorb any calm and rational thoughts from any being.

The left eye of mine twitched with a stitch of pain running through my brow. I was feeling the anguish of silence. "How did you know my whereabouts?"

Sloshing of liquid reverberated throughout the refrigerator as Theodore retaliated, "Is that really what you want to know? Or do you want to know why you haven't died yet from your heart?"

The lower lip of mine writhed with pain as my incisors clenched it with poison taking reign of my veins, "Yes, why am I still alive Theodore?"

Saliva clicked along with the jitters of his lower jaw, "It was the death of one of the nightmares. Did you feel it? Once you took the life away your body was jumpstarted. Well lets say empowered by it. For some reason the artificial heart you've been given reacts to the spirit of it. It absorbs them. Isn't that exciting! You my friend will die still, but with each nightmare's death you will grow stronger and thus have abit more time."

A pounding erupted within my chest, "If I'm getting stronger then why do I feel weaker? And why would the creature that follows me around want me to kill these things if it makes me stronger?"

The smell of vomit and baby powder exited Theodore's mouth, "I'm glad you asked! Maybe with each death of them each one grows stronger... or something like that... and if you rid these things away maybe a peace could emerge from each side and us live together in harmony."

I felt the cool sarcasm spill from Theodore's words but at the same time the idea had practicality and motive. I could propose this to THEM and try to make a deal in order to bring some kind of peace. All sounds easy, but first I must find some kind of leader and do so without dying in the process.

I perform a cathartic exercise to parade my senses to shadow any form of depression. My breath executes small demons that inhabit the vocal famine in my heart. The soft bleat of my heart bounds against my chest in weakness. My body shifts without my commanding leash and I sting with the cleansing drainage of adrenaline through my pores. My soul is tiny fragments of sand passing through a narrow entryway of glass as it speeds up time, the moral deception.

I found my exit, or they did. I traveled with the fatty tissue excavated from the dead beings of the courtyard. They told me it was the only exit, even the dead are not allowed a safe passage from such a structure. I bathed in the seeds of smoldering plastic mixed in peach stomach acid which planted itself into my nasal passages and refused to relinquish control. This waste is placed in a large ceramic tub that is joined with a two foot in diameter hole leading to an abyss. At the moment the tub filled entirely a vacuum begun removing all the garbage, I along for the ride. We, the innards and I, found ourselves happily coating the asphalt outside a daycare.

The air warped around the daycare saturating the color from the ground up towards the heavens. Dangling thirty feet over the daycare was four human bodies sewn together at the heels of the feet and rotating clockwise under transcendental meditation attached by a nylon rope anchored overhead to a floating clot of dirt. The bodies flail in a uniform motion as slits in their wrists shower the beings red blood cells and plasma over the daycare in variable motion. The cloud created in human flesh and feverishly drawing the principles of Newton's law feigned God's want with a captivated wave of the wrist and palm.

Theodore ventured out in another direction opposing mine to find the whereabouts of any of these nightmares. Stemming out from my inner core I felt the un invigorating sense of degree failure. The muscles attached to my ligaments refused to cooperate with my mind's will, my body remained plastered in the mattress of fatty tissue. Frustration is tranquil when it comes to the loss of mobility. It is as if I have lost the pleating in the fabric of my life and everything has wafted into the looming breeze of the night air. I would be dead watching the passage of time across a now nerveless consciousness.

Across the brim of several huffs I cracked the surface of my frustration and peeled my layered pile of flesh off the floor and erected myself. Bonding with my skin the fatty tissue in need of a vessel clung in a deceptively loving fashion as rejection pried it away in waves of heat.

From a cross sectioned wall of the far end of the daycare female screams arose with striking agony. The glimmer of innocence reverberated down from the heavy set musk in the air warping the currents causing a standstill of all air flow. My right arm embraced Sty clenching it to my hipbone for support as a morbid curiosity and dumbfounded want fueled my body to cross the breathing pavement.

Each step upon the concrete pavement closing into the Daycare wisped tiny moderately loud forced exhales from their compact solid matter. Each blade of grass over hanging the edge of the path revealed three inch metal nails camouflaged by the grass holding each blade up, its second purpose. A child sat in the grass beside the wooden fence bordering the backyard of the Daycare, she wore a pink dress with a princess cartoon character sewn into the fabric. In her hand the little girl held a little boy's severed hand as she used the fingers as crayons coloring a human flesh picture on the fence. Her legs were crossed beneath her and impaled with several nails but she showed no pain, she just continued to color.

The front door of the Daycare was nothing but a splintered piece of wood shaped like a snow cone with a handle in it. The music of a deep voiced man saying "Ah hum deeedlee dumm" over and over again squeezed itself through the cracks of the Daycare. The sound of another scream from the same woman rocked its way out of the Daycare's walls.

My finger tips moistened with anxiety as my hand reaches out to open the snow cone shaped door ahead of me. With a sudden spill over my legs arises a lucid static charge that hinders my very stance from alteration. The tiny pulsating beads travel up through my marrow and streaking out through the middle of my shin. I compressed all spiking spurts of emotion in my cerebral cortex and focused my attention elsewhere but this did not come without a price. The price I paid was while each leg ignited into festive strings of knots boggling me down I was distracted from the sinking of the structure ahead of me. The building sunk inward five inches causing the door's end to reach the top of my occupied space.

My palm tingled with a new force that I have never experienced. I felt as if there could be some foreboding reason I should run from the daycare immediately, but here I stayed. Here I stayed to welcome any new event my way.

A soft small padding wrapped itself around the three last fingers of my right hand. I warped my eyes around a vision that enlightened my soul. The little girl whom had been playing by the fence was holding my hand. She stood beside me unafraid. She must not be able to see the kind of beast that lingers near or else she would be running away screaming. A tenderness shocked every muscle in my body, her emotions illuminated a delicate side of the world I don't remember seeing.

A ripping sound scarred the tone of the moment as my black heart frayed. The thread that made up such an organ had been knotted well enough to baffle any being, but this little girl started to solve a puzzle that continued to knit more and more complex patterns. I felt the organ cough a few times as the sickness dampened the blood cells with a black sludge. Even as her hand touches mine with a compassion I've only dreamt about, the darkness in my soul tries to overwhelm all outside influences of honesty, compassion, and love.

"Do you have a home?" The angel below me greeted the dark cloud over head with the vocal chords of pure untainted innocence. My senses flourished with bliss as my eyes devised a way to get my tear ducts back online.

My words could not be found, somehow they found a cabinet and hid in the back where my arms could not reach. I chose not to frighten her with my emotionless screeching and shook my head in the universal form of "No".

"You're always home when you're with people who care." Her lips formed a semicircle upwards as she displayed the uncloaked sincerity of friendship.

My face felt as if it had started melting ahead of me but that was the sorrow spilling from each pore so that this foreign emotion can be absorbed. My eyelids flew at half mast over my eyes to block any signs of pure enlightenment. I still chose to cover my tracks and compile all my emotions inside my condemned cerebral cortex. My fingers twitched with anxiety as I strained myself from not clutching onto her fingertips. I remained shielded in a deepening hole of depression.

"We have been looking for you." Her little tongue flicked out in a zealous fit.

My words hissed from between two clenched lips and a set of bore down teeth, "We?"

Her little cheeks spread making way for her lips to open spewing forth a gentle enthusiastic smile of all teeth, "We are here, not in this trap but we are here. Let me show you."

When she said these words my entire soul lit up like a candle. I flickered back and forth with each hiccup of my heart. She had struck a tune that has never been played inside this concert hall of flesh. She led me behind the building across a patch of grass that did not have the traps aligned with each blade. The backyard shifted from its previous dreary glaze as the little girl set foot upon a dry circular dirt patch. Seconds after her miniature feet tapped the soil she reached out and grabbed my fingers again tugging me onto the patch also. Like an elevator the patch sunk into the earth revealing a hole barely big enough for her to enter. A cold flash of worry secreted itself from my facial pores as she continued to tap her feet causing the dirt patch to sink further into the ground bellow.

Once the patch refused to move any further and my pupils adjusted to the darkness I witnessed a wide open cavern filled with junk confiscated from topside all piled up into houses, and fences, and used as tools by children. The children looked as if they were no older then eight years of age. Each child wore their hair either completely long, cut extremely bad, or had no hair what so ever.

"Haww!" A boy with a sporadic Mohawk eyed the little girl I stood next to and approached after howling for the others. The boy wore no shirt but a gym bag strap around his shoulder and stomach, in his hands he held a whip. "Lucy, what did you do?"

The rest of the children rushed to this boy's aid with weapons, badly made metal spears, and one boy held an aged revolver. Each child had some kind of strap strapped to one part of their body. I easily understood that was their rank in their child society.

"We were waiting for an adult… to… to replace Lionhead." The girl I followed down was named Lucy. In front of the leading child she cowered and became a shelled being, unlike her former self she showed me. Her fingers slipped from mine. This enraged me.

"Haww." The boy squawked at Lucy with anger and hostility as the veins in his neck stiffened and projected out from his body. "Look again at Lionhead." The boy's arm jetted out to his side pointing directly at a staked propped up decaying man wearing a plastic lion mask over his face.

"But he showed us this. How can we live without another?" Lucy raised her hand and clutched onto my fingers once more. The rings of bliss lined my throat with helium zeal. I cringed choking back fasting laughter.

"Haww, that is my job Lucy, we all said so." The little boy's face leeched the rest of the pigment from his blood and interlaced it with his skin cells causing his flesh to glimmer a deep red. "Don't make me teach you a lesson again."

My body tasted the water of curiosity and the sweet bitterness of it begged me to leap in as I submerged my entire presents in the wonder of this little girl's "lesson". The eyesight I've relied on all this time has never stirred me into a wrong congealed emotion. I used my muscles in my neck to help guide my vision towards the little girl's back to check for scars. I tried not to over react when I saw the wrinkled skin of past events formed a line down from her right hand shoulder and behind her clothing.

The hands of mine lashed out and raised the little Mohawk boy by the throat and I divulged him into a new set of leadership, mine. The wisps of my tongue was an awl creating holes of information into this wooden child. "Little hear my name and live. You child might steam in the same rotting pile of bodies labeled property of Blink."

The Mohawk child kicked at me trying to regain his breath as all the speared young souls stepped back in a daze of lost leadership and surprise. The miniature body holding the revolver did exactly what he was told and protected his leader by closing his frail fragile eyes and pulled the trigger.

I smiled, the only thing I could do. The child gasping for air turned a pale peach color when he felt the warmth overwhelm his stomach and drip across his legs. This wasn't a first for me. I relished the draining red lubricant across all my outer nerves. I have become a festive toy for the parading children around me. This blood was mine.

The old revolver had extracted a geyser of one sided rainbow color and had to drill past three inches of muscle and flesh to get there. "Thanks kid." I whispered into the air in my hyped up breathing. The bullet had entered my right lower stomach region and exited the same area taking off flesh and nothing more. I towered above all the children knowing in a fit of rage all could amount to nothing more then a torn page in the Journal of Blink.

I tossed the young child aside and allowed him to regain air into his lungs as I hoisted Sty into the air capping off two rounds which sent every child to the floor wallowing in fear. The barrel of Sty's had become enflamed and I used this to my advantage as I roped both inflamed ligaments into one. The pain was an honorium to my evil deeds for services rendered in the past. Flashes of white light glittered my eyesight as the wound of mine lost all feeling of pain. I charred the nerves from my stomach region. I will not miss these lost tools of feeling.

Bewildered and in condemning amounts of fear each child remained frozen in their fear. Lucy, the angel, was crying with worry beads of pleading peaceful actions. There was the boy with the gun, he had dropped it and covered both his eyes with his salted palms as he cries.

"This world is too much for all of you. This was a mistake for me to be here, this world is not for the children. It is barely enough for me to handle at times. Pray that you don't stick around to see the real monsters on this plain." I rummaged my eyes through the children whom offered tithes of sorrow into the air filling it with a hint of stagnant dew.

Lucy raised up and reached her hand out my way as if trying to call me back in a telekinetic fashion, "You cant just leave us alone… we'll die."

I fastened myself around my first notion, "So will I."

As I speak I am dying. I am taking the last beats of my heart and sputtering out from lack of fuel. I do understand the children's need for an adult and a guardian, but this can not be me. I am a man with an expiration date, I come fractured and defective. They don't want me. I would like for my life to mean something though. If I end up taking these kids lives in my hands and giving them a place to grow, then my purpose has been set. This could be the reason I have survived for so long. I could help these children grow and take care of themselves. But my life will last less then a week if I keep this up. I take in a long deep breath finally counting the bodies in the room. Fifty, fifty children stand around one grown man.

"Blink…" The spout of a familiar voice rang through the back end of the cavern, Theodore. "Ah Blink how did you find the cattle?"

I connected each fragment of my gaze to his bone like head which had little spider like legs springing from the neck cavity. "Theodore? How did you find me?"

Theodore smiled with a devious grin, "You didn't catch on did you? Your heart is what I said it is but at the same time that's how we keep track of you and… where you go."

Vivacious guilt struck me across the collapsed emotions I've buried. "Now you know about the children, Theodore."

Theodore offered a sinister snicker which my eyes descried before it evaporated into the darkness, "Aw, don't worry about these kids. We already knew about them. That's what Lionhead's job was… look after the children. But he didn't do so well and ate some of the berries these little humans gathered and a day later after vomiting up his stomach Lionhead was … dead. I on the other hand just helped gather these youngins and keep them safe. They are our cattle Blink. We've been growing them for awhile."

I listened but refused to hear what this monsters was saying to me. "Why did you keep me alive Theodore? What am I doing?"

Theodore cocked his head to the left as his right spider legs raised up and his left legs took a knee, "Peace. That's all… you see after we started taking over these cattle… everything was peaceful. Only you started killing us. Which was a big different turn for us but we thought we could take care of you. Until that moment I met the Nightmare. That changed it all… I found out there is something worse out there that we have to worry about besides … you. So I decided to use any means necessary to take that Nightmare out. That is why you're still here. Your heart can only feast upon those kinds of creatures, which I believe are part of my race but ones who have transcended into darkness. Ones who have decided to become something else in a sense. So, don't worry about these children … just continue. I do believe that if you end these nightmares then we could work out a peace between us and humans."

I leaned my head back in dismay while trying to rekindle what grasp I could on the situation, "So why do you harvest these children like cattle?"

The spider legs of his crept around making the head seem like its shaking back and forth in a "no" fashion, "Blink, my friend, we don't fully destroy any race. We grow them, they live happy lives. Then when they are old enough to be put down and used we use them. We use them in any way necessary."

My demeanor instantly faded from gray to black, "Then how can there be peace if you use us as cattle?"

"Things can always be changed Blink!" Theodore yelled at me with a stern lifeless anger that greeted the frustrated fabric of my entombed core.

The nails of my hands tickled at my brow as I bounced my eyes between each child gazing each space that could be filled with human beings. Each space was like lymph, resembling one another while occupying the space clouding each important cell of human being. The glimmer of Lucy's eyes caught my gaze of guard and stained itself into the cones in my eyes.

"Options. Many options. One sings out louder then the others. Today will be the beginning of the end. In this chasm our world will thrive. I want the world to know this place, and to fear it. I want your friends to come Theodore, I want them all here. Nightmares will follow, and they will fall. Everyone will hear of this moment and say, between these dirt walls a war was raged, a war to save all of mankind."

A GUARDIAN SPIRIT

    I am a plagued cist of turmoil and liquid want beneath the flesh of a morally impaired rodent. When I step into the light of this world it decays me more rapidly then hiding in my cove of solitude. The stinging itch to flee burns at the soles of my tongue. Why do I act upon impulse? I managed to insult a friend and volunteer these children into a war they never started. If these children die and I survive then who is there to rebuild this world. Who is there other then a crippled being falling apart with every breath? These are the first I've seen in awhile who actually have a chance in this world. Do I put up my life for them? How do I know after I have passed that I've actually done any good?

    God has helped keep me alive. I believe this. I want to. God has helped me stay alive for this cause. Maybe. Maybe I am just a loner floating around being toyed with back and forth while being fickle with my goals. Do I know what I'm doing anymore? No, I don't. I don't know why this couldn't happen to a decent human being, someone worthy of such an action. Am I even worthy enough to be remembered? Who will remember such a dark force, such a demon of society?

    Never second guess yourself. This was something I have tried not to do. I've hurt children, why? I didn't second guess myself. Should I second guess my answer here? I am not sure.

I ended up giving slight nicknames to the children because I have decided getting too acquainted with them would be like harboring a puppy, a burden on my dissolving lifestyle. The boy who shot me I have named Shooter. Lucy has the same name and the boy with the Mohawk I call Hawk. I instructed Hawk to take the children up to gather food and extra supplies for any kind because I had some words I had to address to my friend Theodore.

Theodore and I were alone, I took one of the children's spears and lopped off each and every one of its spider like legs. Theodore was back to normal. Travel sized.

"I know we have our differences. We are of different feuding species. But I would be wrong to admit that you have not been …" I stammered across the sentimental speech I uncovered while searching through my burned cabinets of memories.

"Do you really think you can obtain peace by killing everything?" Theodore used its tongue to swagger its cranium up and over against a rock that lay next to me as I sat next to Theodore on the ground.

The rough gravel of the cavern indented my rump as I paid my senses its toll. The cardinal rule for and society has always been peace, even with the innocence this cannot be sustained. The tin grate behind me crinkled as I leaned against it reminding me of the wall of woe, with all the buried sorrows.

"I don't know anything else but fighting and death," I dampened the brittle matter around with an emotion stained exhale. "My memories have been stripped from me. This place, these children seem like the closest I can come to regaining any type of purpose in this world."

"Desire parades down both sides of the street Blink. Our differences are our likeness. I managed the playground and the souls because I could not destroy. I could not conquer an alien species without feeling some kind of remorse. It just isn't in my blood. That is why I dealt with the already deceased bodies whom I played with, that is why you could not have joined them like you were about to. You would have died. The butcher brought you to me. He was hiding you.

There was a fighting spirit inside of you that just could not go to waste. So I was given the task of converting you. Swaying you from your current path. I've tried so hard so far. I've lead you this way and that but still you find some way to pull out your own positive route. You're really going to take a stand for these children?" Fear radiated out from the tides of syllables exiting Theodore.

I bore my stare into a piece of wood at the far end of the cavern as I slowly nodded "yes", "Do you think bringing everything down here is a good idea?"

Theodore's eyes rolled up to feast upon the sight of my lower mandible, "You mean bring the armies of us and the nightmare down here? That's beyond suicide."

The voiceless choir sings my name while the church bells stifle my respiratory system into breathing through an alternate pitch. Latched onto the burden of the world I stand quaking in my shoes beneath this weight hoping for some other force to save me. Tumbling I find my mind frozen in a time of unmistakable self loathing as I trail behind the green pastures dragging a sponge secreting blood. I am here in sanity's whistle.

"Doing nothing is suicide also. What is a man without a purpose?" I heaved the enlightening reality of my mind's images aside as I sighed.

"Quite peculiar humanity is. You all seem to need a purpose for your life." Theodore's eyes encircled their sockets trying to flex the muscles so they don't stiffen.

"Many are the plans in a man's heart, but it is the Lord's purpose that prevails. Proverbs 19:21" I turned my towards Theodore as I relinquished all my doubts into one momentary glance at a listening ear.

Shooter and Lucy returned through the far end of the cavern carrying nothing as they walked in and laid down behind loose standing sheets of fiberglass which was suppose to be the sleeping quarters for the children. I raised myself into a forward stance as fast as I could but shards of pain sectioned off half of my haste. Shooter laid down with his palms cupping each tiny ear of his as his eyes pinched themselves tightly together refusing all entry of any kind.

Lucy's mouth formed a frown as she crept her knees to her chest in a fetal position.

Heavy footsteps galloped their way towards the center of the room as the force of each shockwave programmed my heart to beat a certain erratic jumble of noise. A composition of extremely high pitched hissing scratched its way through the room as it grinded itself across each metallic surface and back. The sharp outline of a massive figure constructed itself in the darkness as if magic existed. This figure rocked back and forth holding a massive box of some kind as it took a step out from the fog of darkness and into plain sight. It was a creature standing seven foot tall with electrical outlets scattered across its entire body. The eyes were nothing but electrical plugs, and its mouth was the only non electrical outlet entry way into the mass. The creature held a giant boxed television which was plugged into the creatures chest which was the culprit giving off the high pitched screech.

The sightless creature heaved the television to the floor as it kicked up dust in an intrusive cocky fashion. The creature breathed in heavily causing a draft to churn the dust into the cavern causing a stew of heat and moisture. The television snapped on while keeping static the wailing of high electrical pulses. The black and white television revealed a white background and a man standing there with nothing but glued on paper mache. The entity on the screen had a noodle like appearance as he swayed from side to side. The eyes of the creature revealed to me everything I needed to know, who it was, and what it was doing here. The Nightmare.

The Nightmare leaned close to the screen and gazed out at me, "Blink ah good show. Good I am able to find you once more! You almost lost me there. Especially when you were in the prison… ah that was a good spectacle indeed. I feel there are only a few left now. Think, if you finish I will be able to fix you completely."

My eyes formed a point ready to pierce the flesh of this epidemic that blows across the prairie. "You…" Words, they started inside my throat but expanded in the back of my mouth pressing against my tongue like a seesaw causing my tongue to raise and block any escape of air.

"No more words, time for me to show you something. Blink. Ever seen me as a child?" The beast standing behind the television quaked its body as it rumbled to life. The creature reached behind it with its massive hulking arms as it peeled the body of a boy off its back. The young boy's skin stuck to the monster as if it were made of Velcro. Gently standing the boy up in an upright waving position the beast placed the television where the boy's head should be. The nightmare joked around as the television only revealed its head making the image ahead of me appear as The Nightmare was the young boy.

The squire of this young boy's flesh was most noticeably one of the children from the cavern. This boy had no nick name. He was easily the runt of the clan and faded to the edge of the congregation to be invisible. He is no longer invisible.

All the nerves inside my flesh tingled as I lost control of all mobility, Thorns. My knees offered a satisfactory resting place for the rest of my being. I, the kickstand for an immobile land awaiting the persecution of the famine of age starved youth. Goose flesh paraded down my arms while feasting upon all the fear and bitter cold burning from within my soul.

The young boy's arms flailed about with glee as The Nightmare knew youth was sacrosanct to me. The boy turned prancing about with his knees reaching his chest. He tilted his body back and forth trying to find some of the children but the only two in the cavern was Lucy and Shooter.

The Nightmare pierced himself in the chest with a piece of metal tubing that was dropped from earlier by a child. Maroon syrup erupted from the chest and like a sprinkler it cascaded out into the rest of the cavern as he danced around soaking the room in faded life. The dirt refused the infusion of this liquid allowing it to hover above the top layer of rock creating a pool as screams rinsed themselves from the bowels of its sorrow.

A grinding chuckle exited the speakers of the television as my foe laughed. "Children, I know there probably isn't many of you in here right now but you all have to drink from my blood. I know you don't want to but if you don't I will do the same to each and every one of you." His arms outstretched to the heavens, "That's right I feel your woe rising. Give it all to me."

Lucy gleamed in the ball she held herself in, pure innocence. She sparkled with excavated tears radiating her face with fear. She screamed under her breath through the connection of pupils between her and I. I heard her mind beg me to do something, but I could not. She squealed with frolicking furry as her legs just started crawling their way towards the puddle of maroon.

Shooter was already half way to the decaying cesspool of blood when I first laid eyes of him. He was crawling on his hands and knees bucking his head trying to pull away from the power keeping him captive by the electric driven force. His knuckles peeled back his flesh causing his attempts to refuse The Nightmare a chore of self inflicted pain.

Lucy was the first to be dunked into the sludge, her mouth jetting out rancid waves of tormented screams. She was under another beings control as she rolled about in the lubrication coating every external area it could. When her face disappeared within the grime bubbles of unpleasant torment floated to the surface and popped so that the rest of the surrounding world could bask in her disposition.

Shooter lamented me through his watery glare my way. He placed his to arms to both sides as he slid on his belly into the blood. The red welcomed his venture into its island of displeasure. His mouth opened to yell but he choked as a wave of cooling red bombarded his mouth and throat. Shooter's face popped into a bright morose red balloon. His eyes squirted tears into the liquid offering his feelings through manifested creations.

Theodore's mouth quivered as a whisper peeked from his lower lip, "Do it."

I could not move. I had no mobility, no way to help. The heat I've always transferred to Sty to show my control didn't exist either. I was a paperweight whose job was to watch the demise of three children.

A cannon blast echoed through the cavern quaking all the plastics, metal, and wood throughout. The boy The Nightmare's television sat upon lost his right leg and plummeted over along with the television. The hulking beast yanked back on the electrical chord attached to the television as it kept the device safe from harm.

I slipped over trying to hoist my right leg upward so I can stand but still nothing cooperated with my brain's commands. "S… s… stop."

The Nightmare smiled with a devious grin, "Good, some fight in ya."

The beast raised its left leg and stomped into the pond of blood scattering it and flailing it into the air as the creature reared back the television. With a tremendous heave the bulky beast swung the oversized television down from its right shoulder at a diagonal decent. I leaned seeing the object and the path it was taking towards my body as I tumbled my body to the left avoiding the strike. The television merged with its collision course to the ground causing it to erupt with glass and plastic fragments.

I had enough control once again to activate the right arm of mine and initiate it into action. The blood from the deceased little boy coated my left shoulder and left side of my face as I accidentally submerged myself in it. One more cannon blast rocked the cavern which severed the right leg of the hulking beast. No screams exited it as it splashed into the pond of decay.

Still putting up its fight the beast used the massive hands it possessed to pull itself towards my position with haste upon its shoulders. I fumbled with Sty trying to control my fingers as a they moved about in a foreign manner. its right palm crashed down around my neck squeezing tightly cutting off circulation to my brain and airflow. My fingers flickered about erratic and uncontrollable. The outstretching arm or its lifted me high into the air flaunting my imminent demise for the entire cavern to see. My right index finger accompanied by the solid smooth trigger of Sty's severed the chord of the television to the creature as well as drove a three inch hole all the way through the left region of its ribcage.

The beast reacted in pain as it let go of me causing me to take a six foot tumble and impact to the floor. Pain stormed by back as the creature's chord flicked around in front of my face sending sparks towards my eyes. My left hand staggered into play seizing the chord momentarily so I could aim Sty towards the monstrosities head. Unknowingly when I touched the chord a surge of electrical current flooded my core causing my muscles to tense and contract frantically. This sent three rockets into the beast's head and two behind it burrowing deep into the gravel.

The moment came and passed as I let the chord go and removed myself from the unsafe position. The gigantic carcass of the beast rested dead in a monsoon of its own blood. I did not look over at anyone but turned my head to the furthest wall and frowned knowing that the creature was gone, but all the while feeling sorrow that the children experienced such a thing. The death of one child hindered my mind with woe. The Nightmare is destroyed. This was the only positive outcome of the event.

The breathes of mine felt alien. I breathed quickly and feverish. In my eyes a cloud of darkness in the shape of a human being stood translucent and shaky. It was an image of a man completely stripped of skin with a mask of paper with blood painted into a smiley face.

"How curious Blink, some how you have managed to merge us into one body. This will be fun." The Nightmare spread his arms completely wide in a hug type fashion, "We are now one. Lets celebrate!"

Lacerations.

    The dislocation of human feces has come to determine my wealth. I take each problematic handful of human waste and rinse the cleanliness from my core. I the hauteur of self induced havoc reflects the decree of a suicidal parliament. Immoral greed leeched the founding fathers of the freedom pledge. Provisions of freedom can be found behind the scaled walls of society's armored shell. The documentation leading to the damning of millions of human souls takes a minute in a half to read and one moment to sign.
    The world, it is not run by many countries or rulers. It is run by one man, one man whom first exclaimed the notion of making the entire world "Fun". Fun, a word used when talking about playgrounds, children, or adolescents. This word is forbidden when in conjunction with government and democracy, but this man's idea was just. This new idea spread like a plague in the wind, but drawbacks coincided with such an idea. Fun is a term used in one society, not all, each have their own form of fun. This idea did not change the fact that war could be waged for this new idea, a fun reformation of the world. A truer form of failure and meaningless lives lost for a cause without purpose, but this was the reason we were susceptible for a hostile take over. We spread our cheeks as our teeth touched the floor saying

"Insert please doctor." We condemned ourselves to death. Humanity is nothing more then intelligent followers of the dumb.

Energy is from the Greek word energeia meaning activity or operation is the amount of work a force can achieve. The relocation of energy is normal because any energy can transform into another form of energy but always remains the same. This is why through the electrical energy surge through my idealistic cellular membrane The Nightmare was able to break into my cerebellum.

Nightmare, yes I like this nickname for me. Your nightmares are all here Blink, dreams, and wants. How does it feel to know that even in the sanctuary of your own mind, you are still not safe. Actually, I am going to make this the harder battle to wage. Nothing on the exterior will be able to compare with how much agony and torment I can muster while in this state. Greed is what brought you here Blink, brought you to this possessed status. I wanted you to help me. Not destroy me boy. No you had to try to take me down with your ... do you refer to your weapon as a living being? its an inanimate object. Sty, you've named it also! This is going to be a walk in the park. Blink, you are more disturbed then I could have hoped for. I will enjoy this!

Why is this! Stay out of my thoughts! Stay out of my brain! You cant take the only thing I have left and break it down. Why wont you just die? Just leave me alone. Why always me? Always me you had to find to disrupt and plague with your presence. Why?

You're not weak Blink, that is why. I've watched you during the day slaying the innocent and the malicious creatures of the world. You're not weak, you pose a challenge, a threat. So I enjoy messing with you. Just like now. I will gain a high zest of enjoyment.

My body plummeted to the dirt below, once the pain accompanied my arm I started sliding my right temple against the floor in frustration. The spectacle caught the attention of Theodore and Lucy, but Shooter remained distant as post traumatic stress overwhelmed his mind. Tiny pulses of children's feet reverberated through the dirt.

I have to be strong for the children's sake. You can conquer this Nightmare... you can. Take soft deep breaths and box him up deep inside. He is a thought that is all, a memory. What do you do with memories? Do it to him, lock him up. Don't blink, you might miss something. I will not bow and I will not break to this lacerated mindset.

A smile spewed forth from the inside of my cranium and exited my facial structure. The sand stone that use to be called my eyes chafed the sockets they occupied. The children entered the cavern, I on the floor. Concern could be smelt from the air, my nostrils separated the two. I did not see their worry and how they formed a semicircle around my laying pose until I raised my upper torso from the dirt bath. I didn't realize my countenance was still covered with blood and dirt, that was the initial fear the children dealt onto the table.

"I'm okay. This isn't my blood." The puzzled drained quivers in my arms didn't help my explanation towards the mob of kids, "I want you all to pair up and watch out for each other now. No more of this loner straggler stuff. Okay?"

The cracks traveling beneath each miniature foot absorbing the remaining blood whispers the travesty now plaguing Blink's mind. The complexity of this language could not be deciphered by the ears of the children but intercepting the call was Theodore. A squint of damaged emotions trailed Theodore's brow and stung the air molecules around his head.

Blink reached the side of Theodore and rested his muscles next to a friend in concern. His palms outstretched themselves as he flexed them, working the blood back to his extremities. "Place whatever you've brought back in the middle and lets see what we can do with it."

The image of the children piling up the ameba like items had turned liquid with ripples cleansing the reality from the scene. Each ripple compiled the strings of reality and pulled them to distort the images and make each child look demonic with malicious intent. Several children had their mouths gapped open as black tar cascades out from the black hole and down their bodies. The other children had the orbital bone pinch itself into a right angle and add strain on the flesh around it. Blink's mind caught the tail wind of angular momentum's splurge as he became frantically entrapped in a gyroscope of tilled confusion.

Blink's hands outstretched ahead of him towards an unseen object. In the cones of his pupils he noticed a congealing fat that over threw the entire mass of child like entities. The fat tissue pulsed and vibrated with gastric pulses.

The sound of thunder broke Blink from his mesmerized status. Blink connected his gaze to the image of Theodore binding himself with the deceased child. The arm of the deceased child had jetted awake and knocked over a piece of three foot by four foot tin. Blink offered Theodore a secured "Thank you" as normality stained his flesh once again.

"Okay, "the low whistle of Blink inhaling sailed through the cavern. "We will build a barrier outside so that we can bottle neck whatever comes down here. And I will use the entire surrounding area."

A quick cough interrupted Blink as he turned his head towards Shooter. Shooter's lower lip quivered in timid fear. "You can use the ho… tel… hotel next door."

Squinting with a puzzled interested itch of curiosity Blink squared himself up with Shooter, "There is a hotel next to here?" Shooter nodded answering Blink as Blink addressed Shooter once more, "Is it occupied?"

Lucy stepped forward kicking up a fog of dust with her movements, "No!"

Blink cocked his head towards Lucy as he entered a pool of intrigue, "How many are there?"

Shooter dangled his head down towards his chest as he spit out his words, "Enough to kill you."

Lucy struck at Shooter with hatred, "Don't say that!"

Blink fixed his glare on Shooter with the compulsion of being challenged unintentionally. His eyebrows formed into a "V" as his aura bleated out the composite of hostility and security. "Show me."

Through a crawl space I followed Shooter but not before commanding each child to stay put and not to follow just incase trouble flourished. When the crawlspace ended and I felt the acidic glaze of the sun's attack upon the dry desolate surrounding of post apocalyptic caliber. The people whom demolished the town of two story office buildings and immerging fast food outlets. I bore the scab of being a snail under a heat lamp. I tapped into the radio frequency which was broadcasting the image of the chewed up hotel.

    The outside of the hotel steamed with the dried flesh of human beings, intruders. The scaled human remains modeled the diary of their death in permanently entombed pain filled poses. Each body had some kind of gesture reaching towards the heavens, if it wasn't their hands or their heads it was the bow of the body trying desperately to call out to the Lord above, but receiving no answer. Their purpose must have been served, or they were part of the less desirable.

    I could see four guards camping on the roof of the building each wielding rifles with enhanced scopes, what make and model could not be identified from my perspective. Three men camped at the third floor windows two in which were asleep as one played with his Walther GSP .22 Long Rifle. The front of the building had three entry ways but only one wasn't roped off with barbed wire and the staked heads of innocent human beings.

    I tilted my head down towards Shooter which stood directly beside me survey the building. "Seven we can see, obviously there's more inside. You take half and I take half?" I waited for Shooter to respond but got nothing. "I'll take it from here. Tell the others to listen to Theodore. I'll be back by sundown. "

    Shooter galloped back into the crawlspace with haste. His little legs sputtered as he vanished from sight and left me standing alone on the side of the road. I teetered my body to the right and then pushed my feet towards the nearest abandoned store. The front sign to the dollar store had been torn down and piled up and used to block the front door. The entry of the store was barricaded but not long as I launched a brick through a side window and proceeded inward.

    The hour I spent in the store proved extremely useful. I managed to find a large duffle back which I stored Sty to conserve ammunition. I also found myself a knife and a rope. Outside the store I found a 1990

Chevy pickup truck. The people that use to own this truck must have left in a hurry because the key remained in the drivers seat along with the previous owner's legs and entire lower torso.

    I entered the drivers side of the truck and moved the set of legs to the passengers seat. I had to prepare the truck for my escape as I leaned the drivers seat back and tore the back seat out completely along with the back window. Outside the truck I found an unused street lamp that is a good two hundred feet from the hotel so I tied the rope to it. I fixed the other end of the rope to my upper torso and crawled my way through the back of the pickup truck.

    "its killing time."

Blink used the structure of the back seat which had a metal lining to press the gas on the truck after starting it up. The truck gargled with satisfaction as it sped to the front of the hotel. Blink wrapped the duffle bag carrying Sty around his chest. Smoke blasted from the tail pipe as the muffler screamed a war cry into the static day air. Blistering senses, the road warned the force inside the hotel that an enemy is embarking on their terrain.

    Sparks popped across the surface layer of the pickup truck as holes split the aluminum roof open. The sound of many rapid thunderous popping splurged the uninhabited town and bombarded through the truck's dismemberment. Heartless twenty two caliber rounds singed the folded back drivers seat. The front door to the hotel prepared itself for impact as Blink wrapped his hands around his chest and closed his eyes.

    With tremendous force Blink flew out the back of the truck as the rope tensed up completely not allowing Blink to follow the car through the front door of the hotel. Blink's thoracic cage collapsed under the strain of force the rope fibers caused on his cartilaginous structure. His upper seven true ribs fractured and the next three false ribs separated while the two floating sets of ribs breached the wall of pain tolerance in the intercostal spaces as bruising and internal bleeding coated the sternum.

The front of the hotel collapsed inward as the truck barreled through glass and concrete siding along with compressed six inch beams and insulation. The impact tore the metal bar away from the drivers seat which was used to keep the gas pedal floored. The inside of the hotel near the front entryway had been cleared for this type of attack. A cage of scrap metal and tin coated the entry hallway and the booby trap of heavy engine pieces plummeted down from the ceiling and caved in the standing aluminum exterior of the truck.

Pain clung to Blink with enough force to cause black blotches to form in his eyesight. His adrenaline was pumping immensely as he reached his hand up and cut the rope from his chest which allowed all the inflammation to fill his abdomen. Raising up was a chore as each breath and beat of his damaged heart sent vibrations coated in nails through his arteries and into his capillaries. Blink limped while trying to figure out the best way of moving while undergoing tremendous surges of pain through his rib cage.

Blink's right hand used the battered wall of the hotel as a tool to comfort his distress. His eyes shut with compulsion but opened instinctively to take charge in the attack. Around the corner into the building came a Glock handgun carrying .40 caliber rounds. Blink's first movement was to use his left hand and grab the carpel bones in the wrist. His thumb pressed against the Lunate in the proximal row and his middle finger wrapped itself around the wrist and rested upon the Triquetrum also located in the proximal row. His advantage came clear as soon as he twisted his hand the control of the gun for the corner charging foe became equivalent to that of a quadriplegic.

The charging man had hair draping down to his shoulders as he wore a vest of cow hide and blue jeans. The man's hand twisted to his right as control peeled away and his stance became that of a bowed back twig ready to snap. A yelp of pain escaped his lungs as Blink kept his twisting till the man's back hit the floor in pain. Blink placed his right foot on the man's chest and used both hands to keep twisting the man's right arm till it snapped from the socket. Screams painted the hotel with a radiance of foreboding and warning.

Blink ceased the Glock from the crying man's hand and aimed it straight at the human being's face. A moment of moral reflection shrouded his thoughts and movement as he decided not to remove the man's head from his neck. "Not today."

Ahead of Blink came a man dressed in slacks and a sleeveless gray shirt holding a deer rifle the type of the weapon could not be easily distinguished due to all the self modifications done to the weapon. The weapon was raised up into the right hand shoulder of the man's and adjusted to aim directly at Blink's chest.

Blink reached towards the driver side door and peeled it open while the attacker adjusted his weapon for a striking poise. The clap of the rifle burrowed deep into the aluminum siding and metal structure of the door but did not pierce through entirely. Blink used this to his advantage as he rounded the door and clocked off two rounds into the attacker's left leg. The precision of the rounds took down the foe with ease.

Blink hurried his feet to the man's fallen position as he tore the deer rifle from the man's hands. This was a mistake cause as soon as Blink's hands touched the foreign rifle a loud eruption came from beside him which caused a wave of percussion to intimidate Blink and have him cower behind a thin front desk room carved out in the hotel's entry room.

A woman carrying a Remington model 1100 shotgun. She wore black cargo pants filled with extra ammunition and a leather jacket lined with pockets carrying extra shotgun shells. Her bangs stretched down to her chin as the rest of her hair had been cut to a three inch measurement.

Pain complimented Blink for overcoming its messages but the patience it bore wore thin. The shelf below the check in counter had papers which just sat there motionless get up in spurts and just dance about. The image of a fire extinguisher smiling with the tags stating its usage.

"Blink, this is my doing. Do you really think you can overcome me?" The Nightmare's voice echoed through Blink's cranium causing irritation to poison all ideas coming to his mind.

The woman had the shotgun raised up ready to splatter the stranger's flesh across each wall behind the check in counter. She peeked over seeing Blink looking down while scratching frantically at his scalp. Weakness revealed itself as she stepped into view confronting Blink with her presence. Blink jetted his eyes towards her position as he tossed the fire extinguisher into her arms. Instinctively the woman clutched the thrown object with her left free hand. Blink used his Glock to pierce the side of the fire extinguisher and cause the compression of the carbon dioxide to spew out forcing the woman backwards into the nearest wall knocking her unconscious.

Blink raised up seeing the image of her face splitting in two at the upper jaw and her eye lids stretching down over her nose. "You like this one? Can it get you sexual pleasure? Come on for the both of us whip it out!"

"No!" Blink roared as he smashed his face into the nearest wall causing strands of red to ski down his brow.

From across the ground floor of the hotel came a voice that inquired about Blink's presence in a humble peace wrangling tone. "What is it you want? We are not your enemies… please… We don't want bloodshed…or are you just alien to peaceful interaction?"

The Nightmare laughed inside Blink's mind as Blink drooled out a few words, "The Lord watches over the alien…"

The peace keeper tapped his feet as he progressed closer to the back of Blink whom did not care, "So you're a God fearing man stranger?"

A hiss scalped the human tone off Blink's words, "I am feared by men, more then He."

Peace keeper's mouth shut and rejuvenated his tongue with saliva before he negotiated. "Do you really believe God sent you in here to murder your own kind? Is this the work of love?"

Blink lowered his head and turned around to face the Peace Keeper. "God's love dwindles now for a world that rejects him."

The intensity of Blink's gaze stitched fear throughout the Peace Keeper's flesh, "What do you want stranger? This is a colony of good honest human beings, just trying to survive." Blink did not react to the

Peace Keeper's words one bit. "Do you not have an answer for your actions? Did you just desire bloodshed?"

A hiccup of emotion struck out of Blink's nasal passages as he held all reminders of his broken ribs at bay. "There are children, over the way. They need help and a caring hand."

The Peace Keeper squinted while examining the eyes of Blink, "You did the right thing but in the wrong method. But I don't blame you, in these times I would have assumed this place to be a raiders encampment as well. We have used our dead to scare off intruders."

A glimmer of salted liquid glazed Blink's eyes, "Are you all human?"

The Peace Keeper seemed insulted by the question as he nodded. "Yes, I ... don't get why we wouldn't be."

The bland emotion dry tint surfaced across Blink's facial tissue. "At the day care, below it in a cavern are fifty some odd children. I am not anything that can help rebuild. Don't tell them I've left, don't tell them anything. Just let them know that the future is brighter now. I don't know my path still but it all seems so clear now."

I was mistaken. This seems to happen a lot to my fraying mental status. My heart still dies or does it? My chest screams in anxious hymns of pain and freedom from it. God hasn't been able to reveal my true reason for being on this plain and why I am still living, breathing, moving on. The hand saw used to cut through this block of wood called life is dull now. I experienced love. Something of that nature, or I believe it was of that nature. Actually it was more of the lines of security and friendship but I still enjoyed the company. I feel my flame is fading and will soon be snuffed, how can I reap the joys this world has to offer in such little time? I've got a job to do. This job is the only thing keeping me going. I have strayed from the job for so long. My initial reason for survival in this bleak under toe of a world was to destroy the invasion. I've done little to accomplish this goal. I've gained a hole in my heart, the demolition of my memories, and the lacerations on my flesh. So be it if I die venturing forth to oblivion. Oblivion will be my sanctuary and it shall welcome my company.

Good bye worry, so long goals, and welcome my destination. I will walk straight into the heart of the city and call forth a wrath that can only be measured by the buckets of blood. No more trying to find the back door to THEY'RE command node. Let me go to the heart and cut the throat of their president. His body will change but his face, that has always stayed the same.

Symphony of the Dead

    Appraisal is my sought after effect, the cause to this meek venture into the unknown. I own humanistic architecture but cognitively I am impaired. The metaphysical perception of this world I hinder in my post mortem compilation of events. My soul is a vacuum unable to interpret the mechanical vibrations presented down from heaven. The glass in my bones have fractured creating the ripple effect of depression and dissatisfaction to remove the chemical bond between my mind and my body.

    Persistence is the key for a lucrative ending for the ineffective proprietor, me. All goals, all wants, and all desires have an end. The direction all men end up pursuing is the chance to reach the satisfying demise of their life. Purpose in this world is nothing more then a definitive point of mediocre camouflage hiding truth of meaningless simplicity.

    You burn for me, as I burned for you. This is the last line in my Bible. This is all I've experienced. I am being crucified like my Lord. I will not become famished as I juggle the notion of find hope in this world. I may have seen peace, seen a shining splendor of good. But, this is just a fluke. This world has been painted black with decay and agony. When I die, I will be alone. When I die.

Gazing upon my body as I sit in the shadow of a boarded up bathroom wall I resemble a man riddled with Parkinson's Disease. Tremors of pain rock my foundation with little understanding about the shattering psyche of mine.

When I say president referring to this race of creatures I mean the sole commander in charge of each drone of their invasion. He is out there, this tactical commander. The only way I can find him is through one beast, Hermes. He is the messenger and is a driver for the town I refer to as Underworld.

My body must be prepared for such a venture but I unfortunately am not. I will bind my chest with anything I can find and go forth into hell.

I walked across the abandoned city with ease by staying in the shadows. Each step I heard my heart sputter and cough to the rhythm of the inflammation jolting my nerves. The progress towards my destination flew by as my attention poured into my injuries and remained off the patter of my sponge like feet. I did not notice the dimming of the foliage and the darkening of the heavens. Over the Underworld the clouds have formed a black to lime green barrier blocking the sun from reaching the land below. The clouds look as if they are reaching down trying to claw the flesh off the face off the Underworld.

The invisible tug of desire drug me to the moist concrete of the outer layer of the Underworld's only road. The humid smell of demise roasted the incoming particles of the outer world. A brush of death's luring scent drifted in from the wings of a floating piece of decaying flesh. Ash dance across the road as the wind embraces it intimately.

Scratching the silence and causing it to bleed was the screech of a vehicle's engine starting up as a paint crippled taxi cab moves from a pile of dismantled car parts and over turned rubble. The headlights cracked the shell of darkness as the beams peered directly into my soul. The beams bore witness to my hatred, my fumbling faith, and the goals of a wicked damaged heart.

The damaged taxi rolled slowly up to me while the wheel's hammered all objects in its path. Slowly the cab rolled directly ahead of me as the purple glazed tinting on the driver's window rolled down an inch. A river of white smoke cascaded from the inner sanctum of the cab. The window sunk further down the driver side door. The dashboard of the cab illuminated red as the cab driver, Hermes, turned to gaze out the window and interlock eyes with me.

Hermes was eyeless and had no gums or teeth just a black open hole with lips. His face was situated in cringe of anger and animosity. "Hi."

I clutched my ribcage as I gathered up enough air to address the creature. "Hermes?"

A demented grin composed itself across Hermes' crippled cheeks. "I guess you wish to be ferried into the heart of hell? Choose your poison… Where in this town would you like to go?"

My nostrils flared as a stench of decomposition painted the air with the wind as a brush. "Where could I find your … president."

Hermes had his eye brows stretch down to his cheekbone and press against it in a blink. "What? The president? He doesn't live anywhere around here…"

My right hand glided itself across the smooth fabric of the strap around my chest holding Sty. "Not our president. Yours."

His eyes widened in ecstasy, "Well hello."

The back door of the driver's side opened up and the inner light illuminated Hermes as his skin turned burnt and gray like sun bathed flesh. I sprang my feet against the side of the road and with a momentary pause I slid my body and baggage into the back seat of the cab. The door slammed shut on its own as the red hue from the dashboard stained the dark interior and outlined the body of Hermes.

A hearty breathing vacuumed up the musk of the backseat and used it to compose words, "You know you're not the first to come around here asking for the president. There has been a lot before you and will be a lot to follow." The cab started moving along the road at a steady pace while Hermes plucked at his own vocal chord. "Just examine the back seat. You will find some pieces of people from the past sewn up to make a rather comfy chair."

I glanced down to see the fabric used to create the backseat was actually particles of human flesh patched together to create the leather elasticity of the seat. The cab started to pick up speed as the exterior raced away from the sight of Hermes and his machine.

"You will like this predicament." Squealing above the roaring of the rusted engine Hermes swerved the vehicle quickly around objects littering the road. The tires slid across the concrete with burning rubber sticking to the surface as the cab nearly collided with an unoccupied sixteen wheeled vehicle. "You cant hurt me … Why? Cause then we will both die!"

The inner pain of broken bones and frustration merged together in a pact of wild fury, "You have no idea what you're hauling! This machine is not hardly capable of stopping me while I am accompanied by Sty… take me where I want to go, and you will live."

Laughter escaped the roof of Hermes mouth and the mold from his lungs saturated the ceiling of the cab. "Alright lets talk about death and pay it a visit!"

I started to blink as the clutter in the street started to bind together causing little passage. I did not worry, I braced for impact.

"There's a black eye waiting for the sting of rage. There is a dead wish floating in the sun today. This is the same breath of yesterday draped in the untitled voices of those who pray. Prepare to be in pain. It is the only thing that ever comes back again." Hermes recited a nursery rhyme he made up on the spot as he dashed his hands across the steering wheel of the taxi.

Directly centered in each pupil of my mind's eye was a mans face with pockets of mucus seeping and dragging his flesh down and off his face. The hair grew from every pore and submerged his face in hair drenched in flesh fragments. The face moved along with the voice of the Nightmare as I felt his voice flowing through my imagination. "Blink, you always seem to get yourself into the dumbest of situations. This could have been avoided. Let me give you a bit of information to stop me and you from dying. Lean over and whisper to him… Life ends but what we can not see is ever lasting."

Deep inside my chest a little rope pulled and screamed for my mouth not to open but it did. "Life ends but what we can not see is ever lasting."

Hermes appearance ceased to be aggressive as he halted the vehicle next to a hollowed out building which use to be a track of town homes. "Where did you come from? I haven't heard from you in some time. Crete. How did you get in that body."

I squinted with shock as my damaged psyche put the puzzle together, "My nightmare's name is Crete?"

Idling in the middle of the road Hermes turned his head towards the passenger seat while his mouth opened and shut. "Well I guess this makes us friends. I would think Crete would have chosen a bit more of a formidable opponent for the president."

On the interior I sputtered panic around nerves as I tried to rekindle information from past events. The nightmare of mine never tried to hurt me. He would always follow me, watch me. He wanted me to somehow bind with him. Why?

"You know Blink, as you think I can hear I tall. This is my world now. You own nothing. I just have to seize your body and then I'm in business. I have surveyed many worthy candidates to be used but you have something there that just makes up all the right components. Together we will kill everything that keeps Them here. Just so you know. Hermes here is on my side. Yes, he is something else, not one of Them." Crete used my own vocal chords to speak aloud so that Hermes could hear.

Hermes smiled wide as his head continued to still be in the same position and I surged all my muscles with adrenaline as I regained control over my mouth. "What are you two? Why do you wish to take Them away?"

Hermes raised both hands to the ceiling and started tickling it with his fingertips. "I and Crete are what you can call Viruses. We feast upon others. This is all I am permitted to say without being divulged entirely. There is always something else watching and waiting for me to slip up and say something I will regret. Right Crete… Let us head to the president's tower."

The overwhelming flush of new information had caused a dilatory response. "You two are demons. That is the only way to explain it. But demons cant harm the living. That is why you need drones to do it for you. This is the purpose for me. My body."

Hermes coughed up phlegm as he cleared his throat to talk. "No, stop thinking the God aspect right now and try to think logically. Try to think outside of the box. Think about the other side of things. Mirrors show what? Your reflection but not your alternate, we come from there including all the viruses in the world also. How do you think things like that arise? We bring them when we cross over. Now get out of the car."

The pierce of hostility broke the skin of tranquility and conversation as I holstered my initial wants and needs to perform exactly what Hermes asked. Only if Hermes knew that the bag I carry holds the death of anything in my way. Absorbing all noise my body squeezed out of the back of the Taxi with ease. My feet touched a solid surface that hissed at my presence.

A sound grinded through my mind as I stood in the middle of a placid road. The only visible object was a neon building littered with bullet holes. "This is the Killing house. He is in there. Go in and end this."

The Nightmare's voice inside my mind angered my body to the core. At this moment I thought to myself and paid no attention to The Nightmare. What if I kill this thing? What will happen? What else do I do? Maybe there is no reason for me? This could be it, I could try to let them kill me in a blaze of glory. I should just let them take me. I hate this thing in my head. At least it will not hurt anyone anymore. It will all be over. But what about the men at the hotel. They did not understand when I spoke about Them. Them. Do they even exist?

I pulled down the curtain to my soul and all the emotions of my inner sanctum released themselves. I cried, I soaked in a down pour of rain and depression. The diamonds of mine cascaded from my tear ducts and accompanied the rest of the Earth below. It is time to die my friend. Those words echoed inside my cerebellum as I pulled Sty from the duffle bag.

Each step closer to the door of the Killing house I noticed that images started coming into view. To my left was a row of women chewing their right arms off, one was already to the nub where her bicep should have been. They all seemed happy with the lessening of their bodies. To my right appeared a waterfall of men trying to chew their way through the unmoving boundary of water. Their teeth had been eroded away as blood trickled from their gums.

The door knob seemed like it was walking towards me as I remained perfectly still. The knob called my name with unseen lips. The lips lashed out with a noose until it wrung my neck and brought me into the judgment I deserve. My palm sweat shook hands with the cold of the knob. An instant passed as the door squealed from being turned and pushed open. Unhappiness and fate peered through first before the door opened all the way.

Inside the house my eyes devoured the sight of a normal household. The house appeared to be completely normal. Nothing screamed "Evil" or "Death". The house invited me further in as my soul crossed the threshold and then my body followed. The sound of happiness vibrated passed me and through to the other rooms of the house. Zeal poured from the ceiling as everything glistened with bliss.

"Excuse me. Can I ask why you are in my house?" A voice roasted my heart with shock.

From a far chair overlooking the front door a man sat dressed in a maroon robe. I sentenced this vision to a reconfiguration of my senses but still it remained the same image. The man sat comfy in his chair.

"Why are you in my home?" The man's face teased the emotion of hostility but remained calm.

"W… where is the president?" My vocal chords sung a tune of hurt and readiness to perish.

This man's face crunched down on his lips causing a smile to sheer the face in two, "You are another to fall for this. You do realize that these new creatures are nothing more then mutation. This is just the natural order of life, especially after the disasters of today's weapons."

The speed it took for my heart to spew blood through my system raised, "What do you mean?"

The man's left index finger raised up and directed itself to my position. "Let me guess… you believe that this change in human behavior and some oddities of today's society is the cause of some alien race that has descended upon us human beings and proceeds to rip us apart. Such a naïve individual. You do realize this is a trap we have devised to prison those whom have murdered our kind, the infected kind. We have just had peace, that is all. I have helped create a world of peace and now we all abide by one rule. That rule is simple, don't harm one another. Why couldn't you be happy in a world without violence?"

I snarled as I gargled my words, "Why have I seen many human beings suffering? Especially after violence is suppose to be prohibited."

"Please, the only ones whom are hurt or harmed in any way are those whom have chosen to hurt and harm others or even themselves. We are not the bad guys." The man's head wiggled up and down in a nod.

My eyes circled the room with several glances, "Be honest. What are you? Who are you? And tell me about Them."

The man's eyes tilted upward to a clock ticking along at a steady pace. "Okay we have some time. Let me explain just a bit. We are nothing more then just the after effect of a virus. Its just one of those evolutionary traits that keeps us as a race moving. You are just a simple artifact from the previous unaffected few. Don't worry though. The virus isn't really physical. It is mental. Peace was so simple… take away the only reason people have to continue on in this world. Withdraw their God from society and all will just even out. The strange abilities you've witnessed were nothing more then those who have been over run with a peace gene. That's all there is no hostile take over."

Raising with enthusiasm my eyebrows helped stress my thoughts, "I am sorry but sir I don not believe you one bit. I also believe that this thing in my head must be part of your army including the taxi driver outside. Why did you bring me here?"

The man's eyes closed with ecstasy. "He brought you … to die."

A smooth sound of growling etched its way through the front door and into my senses. This sound pinched off all other worries from my mind in an instant. I heard car doors open and shut with force.

Making a face worth peeling off, the man drizzled his amusement from his mouth. "Like I said, it was a trap."

Interest persecuted my mind as I pulled back a curtain and gazed through the window at fifteen heavily armed creatures dressed specifically in heavy duty equipment. The darkness of the exterior shadowed the physically attributes of the newly added figures. I let the curtain rush to its previous position as I cocked my head back at the man in the room. This must happen a lot because the reminder of bullet holes accenting the outside of the Killing house scabbed the importance of my mind.

With a quick twitch of my left eye I could finally feel the presence of God once again empowering my body. They are destroying the Lord. They take what morals there use to be and smash it into pieces. I am here on this planet still to change all that. "I don't know your name, but you will know mine. Blink. So let me tell you a rule of mine which you must follow. Don't blink, you just might miss something."

RIVER OF FLESH.

    Goodnight my friends, these hands I've watched grow. You've done nothing but save me and once again here we go. I have turned multiple times from the good things I could have been. I've walked into this trap, so tell me what time is this? Is it time to trade my soul or use the fist? Tell me hands if I cry, will I fall? Must I depart from all emotion so that I can attach myself to something higher? Oh my friends I have come to savor the beating of this body's drum and I must declare a fault for not caring enough for your needs. The sticks have been broken across my back but I stay wanting more, this my body pleads. I can't remember the shinning star of my past. The scars are the only things that last. I greet this moment with an unsung song. I greet all tonight with a tap of fear. Nothing more. Nothing more cause there's nothing here. These muscles quiver with the strain of age as my mind dwindles from each diary's page. The book of my life is reaching the last rare pages and with these last breathes I can muster red will fly. The dead of this day will offer refuge for those whom seek vengeance. I will show them just what one man can do when he's got a heart full of light. So to my friends; Sty, my hands, and the heart that has never quit I say goodnight.
    The cringe of my stature gleams at the resting being. "Answer me this before all hell rains down upon this building. Who are you? It

seems like you must mean nothing to Them because you are easily at my mercy. So what is your name?"

The man's nostrils flared as he gathered in enough air to send his next message to me. "Alright you have a few moments. I am Eagle Man. And these are my troops here. I am a commanding general in ... well what you call us "THEM" ..."

A compilation of rising pride and anxiety filled the chasm of my cracking heart. "You are telling me that you... are actually someone special in the invasion?"

Eagle Man bit down on his lower lip as he beamed a slight worried glare my way. "Special has a lot of terms but yes. In ways."

I turned fully erect towards the door holding Sty in my hand tapping him to warm him up. "Tonight my friend we will start a river of flesh and leave dying for another day. "

I heard a click from outside. Muffled voices proceed through the solid mass of the door. My hand was outstretched feeling the sound waves break through the flesh and into absorption. I felt their words. A buzz of splinters and wood fragments tickled the brim of my left earlobe.

The fire fight started.

With immediate impulse I ducked my head as I threw open doors behind me which were doors to each closet in the hallway while I headed towards Eagle Man. I tried to add to the amount of objects breaking the path of each round. The rounds turned the entire room into a fireworks show as every artifact within the room sparkled into the air with beauty. My pace was incredibly quick as I connected my left shoulder to Eagle Man's upper mandible. This impact between both worlds sent him, me, and the chair toppling backwards as the bottom of the chair added to the protection for me and Eagle Man.

The stone wall directly beside my head started to crumple as the dilapidated bricks rocketed into particles of sedimentary shards. The top of my scalp tickled and itched with scratches from the claws of the brick pieces. The knitting threads of pain created a quilt of annoyance down the back of my neck. Splashes of solid matter covered every inch of surface on my back. I shielded Eagle Man from being covered in his own trap's fecal matter.

A grunt of force exited my chest as I roped my fingers around Eagle Man's triceps and rolled him and I from the chair's sanctuary. I used the circular motion of my body to hurl the Eagle Man from my grasp and to the farthest side of the room towards another room of the house. Eagle Man flew across the room inches from the hard wood below him. His body avoided every stray bullet flipping throughout the interior of the household. When his body impacted the floor and skidded across to the peach painted far elbow entryway of an adjacent room he finally came in contact with the torment of being impaled with a ricocheted bullet in the left thigh.

I reached into the cascading debris around my head and grabbed a nice sized intact brick. This was my chance to stray the direction of the barrage of bullets. I tossed it with fierce intensity towards a far window on the left side of the house. I demolished the window which caused the wave of metal to stray and give me a moment of safe passage. This moment lasted as long as it took me to step ahead of my current position as the floor cracked under my weight. The introduction of such a sudden jolt of unanticipated events caused my body to quicken the pace but in a clumsy state and I fell forward feet from Eagle Man.

The tremendous boom I caused as my flesh collapsed against hardwood alerted all the guns my way. A fire of plaster and wood fogged the area around Eagle Man and I as I grabbed his leg and hauled his inflamed left thigh along with him down the blazing hallway. Sparks illuminated the way as I couldn't help but to blink continuously at a hyper speed sending the entire ordeal into a slow motion slide show.

I found a door leading to what I hoped was the back of the house but I was wrong. The door knob was cold to the touch and the air outside was stagnant, but this mattered little as blind heated metal searched for my flesh. The door popped open with my turn of the handle. Inside the door which comfortably formed a well balanced shield from the lost rounds of ammunition. The room contained forty hooks holding slabs of human flesh moist and shaved off once living human beings. This room was for processing. The human flesh clothing for Them to wear.

Anger sparred with my will to overreact. A tie finished the fight and I threw Eagle Man in the room with all my might. His head clapped with a clear nylon string as up from the floor raised curved four inch spikes. The trap impaled Eagle Man in the face and the lungs. I tried to reach out for any possible way to secure his life in the hollow shell of his but nothing could be done. He was dead.

The death of Eagle Man spirited a build up of untamed aggression. I pulled Sty to the ready as I opened up the reload chamber of his. Easily I could see five more rounds in him. A compound of pressure splashed through my head as I noticed in a daze of blurred vision that my body no longer touched the ground but sailed backwards in the air. An instant bruise inducing collision to the far wall accompanied my back as my eyes focused wearily on the door I once stood by now in shambles and scattered across the dimly lit tiles of the room's floor.

A beast wearing a hat that formed completely with his scalp and looked as if it had faint electrical wires jetting out of it in all directions approached me holding a sticky mine. The creature's head bowed to the left and to the right as it slithered with its body towards me in a stalking fashion.

My eyes struggled to focus as they peered into the ammunition chamber of Sty's, empty. The impact had sent the remaining rounds astray. I fastened my seatbelt readying the departure from this world as the creature crept forward keeping himself in the ready.

The creature's voice was pinched to a whisper that frolicked through the room kissing each draped flesh on the cheek. "You... you ... you... forgot to ... to ... to ... make ready... your... your ... weapon ... before... this... unfortunate ... wrinkle..."

I could not think of anything else to do but delve into my thoughts. I wisped through everything that has brought me to this point. I rummaged through a sandbox of memories that were new, but something odd fell from the dangling threads of my mind. A box, inside the box I read a note.

"In your anger do not sin; when you are on your beds, search your hearts and be silent. For every battle of the warrior is with confused noise, and garments rolled in blood, but this shall be with burning and fuel of fire for those whom do not know the Lord." My hands reached into my back pocket and pulled out one single bullet.

The creature stepped back raising up his mine ready to use it on the being ahead of him. "What is this? Is this ... the ... last ... will of ... of a man to die?"

My brows molded slightly to the image of helplessness and fragility as I knew the path this bullet must take. "Give me this moment. Let me finish this like a man with some kind of honor."

The mysterious creature nodded with a grunt of nostril escaping air.

I loaded Sty up. My best friend knew the reason for this round that has been saved in my back pocket. I pressed the barrel of Sty's to my lower jaw as I tilted Sty back towards the back of my head. "I remember everything."

With one quick pull of the trigger in conjunction with a forward thrust of my arms I redirected the barrel of Sty's towards the mysterious figure's head and pried the cranium from the spine. The violet blood of his sprayed the room with glee as all my memories rushed back into my brain. I tipped the glass over and spilled the memories of childhood and my former family onto my hands as I washed the blood clean. I found my calling once more. I have called the Lord's name while in need and gained a miracle.

My body ached but my soul enlightened. Fourteen more remain.

I stand not for myself. I stand sore but I stand. This body is driven by a different means, not an individual playing with his selfish wants. I am driven by a new focus, humanity. We are human. Human beings desire the freedom we all deserve. I stand to show a lack of compromising to a tyrant or tyranny. This is my legacy and I stand to show that I will not sit by and watch events pass, I did that during my youth. I grew up since then, I am a man, so what I do now is I take the responsibility I deserve and fulfill my moral rights as a man. I will raise up for all man kind.

A headache sets off an alarm trying to rekindle my attention to the world around me. I still have fourteen more strange abominations of the world to smear across this trap's interior. I will be a colorful sight to see, and so will this night.

I timed my body according to the tension of the night, the moment at hand. The clatter of my feet accompanied the presence of another figure of the army sent to rid my face from the scene. The body of the creature was slim but that doesn't matter when it comes to working an automatic weapon like the one he held in his right hand. Once my senses locked on to this thing I could not help myself. My right hand flipped Sty around and with his butt I jabbed the creature in the face causing maroon steam to slip from his nostrils. His weapon popped in his hand as his left hand also clenched itself. His weapon was tilted down at the floor as I crashed the butt of Sty's once more in his eye socket. This impact sent the creature into the wall, I charged to accompany his pain with Sty one last time. I squeezed his brain with the back end of Sty and aimed Sty towards the opposing end of the hallway. I hoped for another demon like being to be standing at the other end but nothing with a pulse occupied the target area. I decided to aim Sty at the front door of the building, this was a wedge like shot through a doorway and across another room and passing two doors whom have been opened for an obstacle reason. Sty helped me on this one as the front door splintered into pieces and the recoil from Sty cracked the frame of the beasts head in two as he slumped into oblivion.

I used my tongue to slurp up the sweat beads collecting upon my upper lip. The taste of two deaths and thirteen more to come. Eagerness for a clever trap to present revenge with wrapping paper and a bow.

Using a two foot one inch wide board I strapped it to the dead creature's arm by tearing its clothing into strands. With haste I also used a spike from the skin room to impale the deceased beast's finger which I placed on the trigger of his weapon and positioned it towards the other end of the hallway. I propped up the arm with its legs and held the strand of cloth connected to the trigger finger.

I quickly realized the two I destroyed were only the scouts, expendable. The strategy of a house raid is let the front men be well trained but nothing that you cant live without. The third body should be a juggernaut or something that has the ability to take down whatever survived through the first two. This strategy was used. I met their juggernaut.

The structure of the house quaked violently under each footstep of the approaching creature. I hid behind the entryway to the skin room and listened intensely. I was hoping to catch this beast off guard but my trap turned around on me. I had controlled my breathing down to a faint wash of mist to escape without even a hiss. This creature must have been blessed with acute hearing because it knew exactly where I rested my back. I had lulled my heartbeat to a smooth clap but it instantly escalated when the Juggernaut plowed through the dry wall behind me and sent me skidding chest first across the ground underneath the skin drapes.

The Juggernaut wore planks of metal underneath each arm on the forearm and had metallic shards pointing out from its leggings that shielded the belly of the creature. The Juggernaut sent a ludic grunt towards my position as his intentions were clearly lucid.

I lurched my body to the right as I climbed to my knees. I feared paresis with the massive beast at hand. The strike alone could have demolished my back and sent my entire lively hood into the next dimension . I surveyed my parameter and enjoyed every bit of it.

I raised completely to my full stance as I left Sty on the floor. I wanted this Juggernaut to marvel at the paragon standing before him. Each receptor of mine refused any part of communication relaying pair of any sort. My stance was to repudiating the notion of my failure against such a towering foe.

I tossed caution into an abyss filled slumber as I charged the embodiment of mayhem. The thundering brunt of my attack doused me into a hornets nest of damage. The moment worked as clockwork, first chime was the Juggernaut's catch of my body. The second being him rearing my fraying structure into the air and third being the concussion I bonded with at the other end of the hallway. The foe currently threatening my being hurled me back into the hallway where my trap is set. This was a risky move of mine and caused damage to the beams holding my sanctuary off the ground.

I used this moment of bliss the Juggernaut retained and crawled quickly to the thread I've interlaced into an automated fate. The Juggernaut stepped directly into the path of the trap I've set. The outlook of the attack I had set up seemed sweet. The glide of my elbow and the pressure upon the dead man's trigger finger created a spread of dread to fill the hallway. A spree of heat drizzled horizontally through the sententious morose musk in the air. Each round of the automated weapon struck the Juggernaut but utilizing its armor plating it repelled each attack without hesitation.

The hulk of muscle started walking through the monsoon of metal. Sparks luminescent with yellow flare flicked about the monster.

With fear prancing through my veins I roped the thread around the head of the corps to keep the weapon firing at the Juggernaut. This bought me some time to calibrate my legs again for rushing to another destination. I hurried through the crumpled doorway and into the skin room once again as I heard the machine gun get ripped to shreds. I gazed down at Sty as I fumbled through an apology. I had been cocky and thought I could handle something alone. I scooped Sty up with my right hand as I crouched down completely trying to peer under the skin apparel to watch the feet of my foe.

I saw his massive feet cracking the floor beneath each pound of his weight. I found a strategic idea flutter though my puddle of thoughts and I used it. I pulled the right hand pocket of my pants out and ripped it open. With haste I also pushed Sty down the right pant leg. I then turned to the far wall seeing a mobile cart carrying sewing equipment. I leapt up to my feet and scooped the cart up in my possession. I made as much noise as I could to gain the attention of the Juggernaut.

The massive swipe of the Juggernaut's arms tore each flesh suit off its spiked hanger. Stringing its glare with mine I pushed the cart through the newly developed pathway. Laughing at me it caught the cast and hoisted it up and immediately followed through with tossing it back at me. I slid to my back expecting the retaliation. When I hit the floor smoothly I reached my right hand into my right pocket in preparation. The Juggernaut felt the passion of victory searing through parched nerves as it used both hands to clutch my right leg.

My chance was now so I pulled Sty's trigger as soon as an opening revealed itself. The head of the Juggernaut hollowed out with one clean passage. Muscle functions and life poured from the crater substitute for the Juggernaut's face.

A sting latched onto my reunited nerves. Twelve more to go.

Hybrid Famine

I don't want to live, I don't want to lead. My desire is to breathe. I breathe the malnutrition of morals back into the world that has condemned its people. Life has damned the world into a moral famine. We suck on the poisonous nectar of a sinful economy. The dimes of prosperity hinder the focus on objects instead of purpose and necessity. The face of the honest hard working man is in a famine also struggling to gain some kind of nutrients out of the coal they feast upon.

Clear strategy, that is the words that describe the attack. Three down, twelve to go. I ache with hunger for nutrition but also moral values and love. I am a complex hybrid of famine. The strategy after such a foe would have to be a mentalist. Behind each bronze must be some intelligent being to follow up and make sure he can control and also take control of the situation. I watched for brains. This is what I call it. The next attacker I called Brain.

My next few movements could be compared to the makings of a modern light bulb. I replaced the ceiling of my room with a hole so I can vacuum out the inhuman tainted air from the above floor. Using the chains I squirmed through the hole and into the next room above while pushing out the old dry air. Clearing out the oxygen in a light bulb is important because yellow and white heat reach temperatures at

3,500 to 5,000 degrees Fahrenheit and basically all known materials react to oxygen and burn up in a few seconds. The wire causing the light shouldn't burn, me. My covert movements following my arrival into the room were enough to create the slow generated amps to light up this bulb of human presence. I radiated like a lantern in a subterranean cabin. I paused to take in the surroundings. I could see nothing. I was being stalked.

It spoke to me. Tried to communicate before it attacked.

This is the discussion between Brain and I.

Brain—"What exactly are you trying to do? I've watched many forms of your kind perform the exact same bumbling attempt to transform your world back the way it was. Failure is the only outcome... What do you believe we are? Your kind creates us into monsters through fables passed about. Do you really know? No... let me explain to you Hero what we are. Your kind refer to us as dark matter, and our presence as dark energy. Regular cosmetology have easily explained the speeding up of the universe as dark energy and have described our gravitational pull from our presence as dark matter. This was an insult, in all reality your kind lives on a parabolic state not a flat plain like you were told to believe. Your eyes could only adjust to us on a mediocre nature when our plain which is flat crosses yours. Well this what has happened is through the induction of fusion power to your culture you have bowed the plain of your existence to a "U" that crosses our plain beyond the average. We are now one. You can not get rid of us, an entire mirror world. This is not an invasion but a merging of the two worlds. Stop what you're doing... just stop trying to harm something you don't understand. You've just become a monster in our world. Does this seem like something you want to do? Did you set out to kill an entire world, Hero?"

I—"My name... is not Hero. I am named Blink. I have not been born with this name. I've chosen it. I've chosen it because those whom have their eyes open ... know HIS glory and grace and have been saved in their hearts. Those whom reject or neglect a higher presence has their eyes shut completely, but those who have bore the burden of sin but still walk a fine line between belief and betrayal, this is normal human beings. We blink. I am Blink. I am here to fix the world by whatever means necessary. I will correct this problem either destroying you, which have already started condemning us, or die trying to avenge those who you have decided to kill in order for you to survive on this new ... plain."

Brain—"Well isn't this fun… someone whom has a mission sent by God Himself. I guess there is no persuading you from your common goal of most human beings. You do understand that in this war … neither will win or one will win entirely. Either way the casualties will be great."

I—"That is why He did not send an army but a single man. Don't you think maybe the idea of a God is a bit more believable then just pure luck."

Brain—"You're a strange being human. Why do you believe in superstition?"

I—"God has punished man one time. And whipped us off the face of the Earth, but now we have lost faith and you have no faith. In order to fix this world we will all have to come together and rekindle the faith. This will save us all. Don't you think.

Brain—"Yes, a commonality could fix the problem but not one that involves false promises and ill facts. We are not a stupid society, we do not war upon each other but are one conjoined unit. We care for each other. We are beyond your kind, murderer."

I—"With the pursuit of heaven always comes the inflammation of hell."

Brain—"Well traveler, Blink. I am glad we now understand one another and you have bought me this time to prepare your fate. I acknowledge that you are not the most intelligent man whose come across my path."

A sudden surge condemned all my sight as I romped through a daydream which told my mind and body to make amends. I was surrounded by golden pastures as a lone translucent spherical prism disguised as a sun beamed out sparkles of hope and happiness. The golden blades of grass puffed varied amounts of pink bubbles into the air as they floated away on visible blue wind blankets.

The malicious intent of Brain snarled from within the darkness of my own fog of war, "Smell for me. What could be surrounding your body in your current state?"

A flicker embraced with a snap illuminated a circular enclosure around my body which was composed entirely of free floating liquid. The liquid progressed in its rhythmic pattern as constant wakes refused to let friction take hold. The top of the liquid boundary was connected to the scaling roof top above.

I bit down on my lip as I chugged a dry brick down my throat. "What is this?"

The voice of Brain seemed fully delved into content, "Curious are we? Well this is actually a quale of reinforced phenomena. Let me explain... what you see ahead of you is your own perception. It is a familiar scene but transgressed into an unfamiliar plain. The ordinarily horizontal spectrum has now been subjected into the vertical one. This is only able to be maintained because of something I'd like to call Floating. First off I've created this cell of yours. Just like the factors of a battery I shall use this liquid membrane to hold you in a Floating Voltage which keeps the liquid barred in a wall like state. I say Floating Voltage cause that is what is running through the walls of your cell, and you represent a kind of floating voltage. Right now your body, your rage builds and is held captive in this prison of yours.

With confusion warping my mind and embodying my soul I looked to within and it spoke to me, the nightmare. "How different we are. You tread the waters of good and evil constantly. I do whatever I feel at any moment, no morality. But because of this, this creature ahead of you. I feel like I should do something good and tell you something you may not know. There is no trap. This is an illusion. This thing has used a special hallucinogenic pheromone that constructed any trap it decided to make up. There is nothing wrong with you. And don't thank me. I'm just wanting to see how far you can actually go. This is entertainment for me."

My mind is a limbo stricken muscle weakening as the weight of the world piles atop of it. It lingers in the chasm of Nastrond, a snake infested hall that drips poison deep below the belly of hell. Here in this state I witness Nidhoggr the colossal serpent owning this hall. He senses my dismay and his appetite swells because of it. He is the encrusted congealed image of my current plight. The poison of each serpent lathers my melancholy skin as the corrosive nature of mine breathes from my stained gravel spewing cerebrum. Famine of my memory from my temporal lobe has propelled my frontal lobe into making very resourceful reasoning while hacking each emotional stimuli into bite sized pieces.

What this Brain didn't know is I have changed my cortical folding and added a few more highways between my frontal, occipital, temporal, and parietal lobe. I knew his attempts would be just, and an illusion. I knew the nightmare would try to enlighten me about the attacker, save me. I knew all of this. That is why I gave in. I let him take me.

I slunk into a fetal stuper as I pretended to wilt into a succumbing status. This proved to be a positive tactic as the Brain revealed himself. The image around me dissolved as I remained hunched and breathing with heavy moisture bearing waves of woe. The Brain was not seen by me but heard. I continued to direct my vantage away from him so that my lack of acting ability could not be quickly established.

"Death is something suitable for all to wear." The Brain tapped its toes on the floor quickly as it approached me.

I cracked some words out from between my lips to try to redirect his actions, "Please, don't let it be here."

Hesitation proceeded as he strained his approaching nature. I could hear a slight squeal of nasal usage breathing in and out as he flared up his brain and tried to reevaluate the situation.

"Too long." I swooped kicking my leg along the floor as my chest revealed itself to Brain. Sty smiled with ecstasy as this creature's bewilderment composed a melody of pure primal decapitated bliss. In a freeze frame of enjoyment my mind took a picture of the eruption of glistening blood from Brain and his cerebellum. His head appeared as a festive frolic of fireworks to me enlightening my soul and enriching my heart with awe.

I hoped that Brain would take me outside and maybe try to make a spectacle of my death so I could end them all. But this only seemed to be a hopeful wish, nothing ever comes easily. I have an idea that has been brewing in my thoughts but I have to have faith that this could work. Faith is the hollowed out entrails of a wooden unpolished and charred soul migrating to hell for the winter solstice.

Before I knew it my body pulled me into a far room near the front of the house. I rested my head upon the wall next to the window. Outside there were many bodies moving frantically. They all held automatic weapons directed somewhere at each angle of the house. I felt a tingle approach my fingertips as they pried open the window. The shimmering sound of the window squawking into the night caused a jitter gun fire on my position.

The rapid miniature explosions from each bullet piercing the wall causing shards of dry wall and wooden splinters to dance across the room as the song of heated copper and sparks dazzled the inner sanctum. I fumbled into a pocket of cover as I waved my hand through the glitter of beauty shattering the glass of silence. The window erupted as it accompanied the rest of the debris in the air and buzzed about laughing with high pitched glee.

The spray of gunfire halted as the sound of reloading stung the air. My body fled to the far right of the former window and under adrenaline filled veins I did not take notice of the copper burning my thighs as I spoke with vigor out the hole and into hell. "You have no idea what you're doing. I will show you something a few people know about. Bring your leader here and this will be seen by him too. You will finally realize a greater power then yourself. Maybe then we can reach a peace, because if you choose not to this higher power will use any way necessary to exterminate your kind. Bring someone to see this. Bring someone to witness this power. Or you will all die."

Maelstrom of Decay.

    The blind can see more beauty then those with sight. The dead experience more freedom then the living. The impaired receive more from their incapability then those whom are capable of experiencing the world in its entirety. I handicap myself with a purpose. I am a driven being seeking enlightenment to bind two foreign parties together. This type of union between two groups has never been attempted. God has never been used as a glue.
    God has been used for death, destruction, and mayhem. The name has been stamped upon wars, murders, and crusades. Was this merely man's inability to get the population's blessing for war, or was it an ill interpreted message sent from above? It could have been His will. But I don't believe so. Man, like any animal wants to be the dominant species, we have a maturity issue. We push aside those whom stand in our way for power and knowledge. Shattering each goal in every person's life will reveal an unbiased truth, knowledge and power are the only reasons for living. Some human beings fight for what's right so they can retain the knowledge of self gratification and receive the power to perform this feat again. Even I, I seek knowledge. Knowledge to know that my life has not been a mediocre rummage through the scorn of this land just so I can die and leave it in the same rubble I found it in. I seek the knowledge of purpose, and if I have to

I'll use the power I've gained from my path to knowledge. I am a killer, I am a murderer, I am a monster, and I am a peacekeeper.

The rancid web of events that latched me into this tabernacle has proved to be a much needed exercise for what I'm about to face. Thank you Theodore, my friend, a friendship built on deceit and puppetries but still a friendship all the same. Lucy showed me a side of compassion I have never experienced. There I was a beast spewing blood wherever I would roam and this young child saw something else inside I never knew existed. I do not regret the Stuttering Prophet and the wisdom he has shared with me, though he proceeded to lead me to my death I still will miss the brief moments shared in his guidance. I see in this web a ticket price to be in this house, that is the body count of experience I have created along the way.

Striking from outside a venomous voice ricochets around the room of mine searching for my ears. "Stranger! Reveal to us ... this ... gift. You do understand we can not endanger our commander's life for a charade. We will give you thirty seconds once you exit the front door to show us this deity of yours. That is the most I can deliver to a mass murderer. Yes we know you are the same man that has been leaving a line of destruction for some time now. You have two minutes to comply before we come in after you."

Chances, they come once in a life time. Chances to do the right thing, chances to save the world, those chances come once in an eternity. This is my chance. I can offer up myself and show the world something this plain has never seen. I can show these two worlds so true savior. The one whom saved me.

I feel a hand upon my shoulder. I feel no worry. Sty in my right hand agreeing with my choice. The door opened with ease as the musk of a generation needing knowledge drenched my flesh. Peace enveloped my inner core pressing buttons releasing hope filled endorphins into my spinal chord. This was it, my true calling. If my cheeks knew how to smile I would have. Here comes the sun.

Lights from the enemies standing across the front lawn blinded the silence of the message endowed man, me. All with a roar of triggers pulled, I painted the canvas of this scene with a violent less hole in the attacker's sternum. Each creature ahead of me tried gunning my body down. Their attempts until now have been futile, nothing could hinder the message I hold.

From inside my cranial cavity I heard a voice lash out as an acid cloud curdled in my mind's eye. "What do you think you're doing? God wont help you here." The nightmare removed what faith I had with a fate slicing twist of a nail into my prefrontal cortex.

Behind the light bearing down into my flesh trying to pierce my soul came a voice writhing in hatred, "Enough of this." A buzz of three lead hollow point rounds stung the air as I felt my upper mandible shatter with a wailing impact. I stumbled backwards back through the doorway and onto the floor with my rationalization frantically dethawing itself from under a lonesome glacier. My nasal passages refused to cooperate as blood climbed with haste through my airways and into my lungs seeking shelter. My vision blurred as a soft rhythmic clatter of sluggish beats drained the sound from the tabernacle.

Dissolving from my eyes was the image of this building being a heavenly place, but I see it now for what it was, a tomb awaiting my departure. My nose had been split in two as my upper jaw clutched tightly onto two of the rounds lodged in my face, as the other round was burrowed deep in my nasal system. Confusion swept away my mobility, memory, and faith. The warmth spewing forth from my face bathed me in my dreams, my love, my losses, and my pain. My dazed state wished for guidance but lost consciousness as it died and I realized they will see the monster inside.

Adrenaline ravaged my core as my presence rose behind the door. In my right hand blazed a heat that erupted into my friend Sty. His nostril's flared as searing red flushed his barrel and coursed into his trigger. All around the room a woe crawled through the chemical bonding of each artifact. I slapped into a craze as I unleashed hell upon the eleven beings outside the house.

Sty sneezed several rounds towards the lights weighing my vision down. Flares debris and sparks composed a sweat of fear to arise in the remaining army. A jumble of blood sprinkled itself into the night's arid sky. Pops of random fire whistled as they struck the lining of the doorway and hid in safety. Sty swiveled and decapitated a few struggling creatures trying to reactivate their weapons. One still had its esophagus still attached and so the flesh absorbed the night's gentle touch.

Finding the opportunity to leave the doorway I did as the blaze of gunfire hurled itself into the structure of the building. The house moaned from the gnawing power of each bullet. I walked without worry to a far window to relinquish some more destruction. The house behind my footsteps wallowed in the screams of chipping and fraying wood.

At the window I cleaned the vantage of mine with a quick blink. Eight stand ahead of me with their guns at the ready. Five bombard the front of the building with gunfire as one sits in a vehicle clutching the steering wheel readying for attack. I could see their leader pointing towards the left side of the house as I unlatched my faith into its command. The leader of the small army ahead of me crashed to the floor as both of its knees detached themselves from its thigh. A parade of pulsing questions breached its head as I lurched the next creature into a splendor of glistening red dust.

The wheelman sitting at the vehicle's driver's seat roared the engine and steered the hulk of metal towards me. I grinned out of want for death and not out of pleasure. Sty removed the creature's head as the windshield crumbled into razor shards. The vehicle continued on its destructive rampage towards my presence. I leapt into the air turning my back to the non existent windshield and as the window and wall exploded from the impact of the bumper. I rolled inward into the front seat cushioned by the dead body of the creature. The vehicle crashed into the staircase as the vehicle's movement ceased giving me a jolt forward out the front of the windshield. My body hit the hood of the vehicle. A haze bubbled over my flesh causing a drowsy feeling to remove my consciousness momentarily.

The sound of approaching feet clattered their way towards and around the vehicle I lay on. In the current state of dreary collision I used my probing fingers to pry my ship into the cockpit of the vehicle.

My cocoon is sore and wilting from the stagnant pain wrangling my soul. The quick patter signaled from the other side of the vehicle's aluminum siding. I ripped out the side casing with a rocket from Sty as the instant rainfall of copper rounds flaked the drivers side of the vehicle into paper.

Croaks from my blood filled lungs caused a foam to arise from my split nasal passages. The creature's weapon snapped as the last round was fired from the chamber. I tried to move my feet and kick my body out the passenger door but before I could finish my attempt to exit the vehicle I found myself being drug through the driver's side and out the door.

Blink.

I saw shell casings intertwined with grass as the grasp on my ankles pulled me by my legs as I was hit with the bump of the sidewalk. The concrete scratched and clawed at the fabric of my clothes. I murmured as blood and saliva sprayed out of my damaged mouth cavity. "I'll show you God."

The creature dragging me halted his progression backwards and leaned in close as his image was jumbled up and grainy from my failing eyes. "What God?"

Sputtering from the injuries sustained in my arm I flinched and sent a compilation of fate and faith through the creature's cranium. His body became dilapidated as it sloshed into the grass accompanying death hand in hand.

I lay alone. The arid badland above me rejects the presence of my breath as the rocky beast below me pets my back with a cold feather. Darkness envelopes my eyes as I hear the world awaken. The slim itch of a cricket dried out within the drums of my ears while the dying song of a bird rummaged its way into my senses.

A barrage of tiny probing finger tips against my external flared tissue. Voices reconciled the issue involving me.

Voice of an elderly man locked in a lisp, "He's easily a loss. Do not touch his body. He has the curse, I feel it."

Contradicting the voice of knowledge was a young woman's whispered pant, "We could use this. Even if it doesn't work we can still benefit from helping this being. What do you think we should do? Do you leave every one of God's creatures left to die. We need to rebuild society not disregard it and let it die."

Without control of my body I heard words exit my throat, "The Lord will fight for you; you have only to be still…The soul of the Lord hates…those who love violence."

Good morning my nightmare. I have been melting inside for some time with you. You can poke and prod my thoughts, my body all you want. It is mine. I have had a momentary loss of faith but God loves those whom have been to hell and back and choose the heavenly gate over that of blood. The leech of faith I've encountered reimbursed me with something more. My trivial lesson is one that demanded a payment unable to be cashed by my hands and thus the debt escalated until grief blistered my cross to bear. I am bare now, nude to my emotions instead of calices covering my heart. I know how to fight you now. I will battle you every day until my body fertilizes the Earth.

A week has blinked across the horizon as my body reconstructed itself the best it could with the help from a colony of human beings. They have fed me, clothed me, nursed me back to health. I saw Lucy, she smiled at me even though I appeared as a monster in the flesh. They want me to teach them more about the Bible. They want me to teach them how I've lived through so many ordeals, caused so much destruction. They want me to guide them to the Lord. Some teacher I could be. I seldom think of Theodore and where that head is at this moment. Could he be changed, helping free this world of war. I wonder a lot now. I have been immobile for some time so my mind would wander through the actions of my past.

I have to pause and derail my ideas sometimes to understand why I am here and why my intentions did not work. I have noticed that I went the wrong path, I tried to take the place of God and be Him. This was my downfall and reason for my pain. But I'm not dead all the same. I have now a reason to live. I have a family. I am going to use them and start a crusade through this world removing this infection from the Earth's skin while using the vaccine of The Holy Spirit. This is my path and this is my legacy.

I chuckle as my heart gives a bound. My enemies quiver as they hear one last sound and see Sty with a gleam in his eye. "Don't Blink. You might miss something."

LaVergne, TN USA
24 November 2010
206098LV00005B/35/P